A HANDFUL OF QUIET

A Novel

KARL RODMAN

Epigraph Books
Rhinebeck, New York

Paperback ISBN 9781966293248

Library of Congress Control Number 2025921792

Book and cover design by Colin Rolfe

Epigraph Books
22 East Market Street, Suite 304
Rhinebeck, New York 12572
(845) 876-4861
epigraphpublishing.com

A HANDFUL OF QUIET

Better a handful of quiet, than both the hands
full of toil and torture of spirit.
ECCLESIASTES IV,6.

CAVEAT

This novel is fiction and its characters are fictional. Historically remembered events are mostly true, both as to chronology and depiction. However, the reader is advised that one major event in the novel is purely imagined. This event should not be taken for a well-remembered but similar event that did occur later.

CHAPTER ONE

WE PARKED in front of a flat-roofed structure and, with my permission, twenty-three fifth and sixth graders erupted from the school bus and milled around until a museum docent appeared and beckoned them to enter. Jostling one another they squeezed through the door of the Trailside Museum. I followed behind, pleased at the prospect of a couple of hours break, during which somebody else would take over my class.

I hadn't come in anticipation of finding a soul mate, although it's true I was always looking. I was nearly twenty-four and troubled that the search, so far, had had given me very few positive results.

The rather plain docent with curly ash-blond hair who greeted my class identified herself as Louella Cook. She was a volunteer in the college's Trailside Museum. She immediately took control. I watched as she explained the exhibits, dioramas, and charts. She opened the animal cages and allowed my eleven-and twelve-year-olds to stroke some of the furry animals. She extracted one of the garter snakes and let it entwine itself around the hands of anyone who volunteered. Once the museum displays were exhausted she said, "Let's go outside now and see how well we do at identifying the plants and trees along the trail." My children followed her readily. I stayed behind and enjoyed the solitude and quiet of the empty museum.

I fully appreciated the free time; no responsibility. When they returned, the docent served juice and cookies. Next, she picked up her guitar, saying, "Before you have to go back to school let's sing together."

As she scanned the pages of her songbook I noticed that behind her large framed glasses were blue eyes. The songs she chose were the summer camp songs of my childhood. My normally rambunctious students were enthralled.

I was smitten.

I was already in my second year at the Lab School: my first job.

The first year of teaching, I had been told, is always hell. It certainly had been for me. The second year was better, but most of the time, in Southern Ohio, far from my Eastern home, I still felt myself in purgatory, struggling to learn how an adult is supposed to live in the world.

The job at the Lab School had sounded ideal. "Come teach a combined fifth and sixth grade, composed mostly of faculty members' children." Here I was, a freshly- minted teacher, possessing a Master's in Education, and suddenly I was a fully fledged faculty member, an instructor in the Education Department of Horace Mann College, Cold Springs, Ohio.

My first year I rented space from a severe, older lady who informed me I was not to bring girls into my room at night.

Unfortunately she had nothing to worry about.

The second year, I became friendly with Jim Krikun, a fifth-year student. We rented a two-bedroom prefabricated bungalow on the edge of the campus golf course. I still wasn't bringing any girls home at night, but having a roommate, I was a lot less lonely.

That evening I told Jim about the girl who had handled my class so well. It turned out he knew her.

He told me Louella had graduated three years ago and stayed on as a teaching assistant in the mathematics department. Jim sometimes dated Louella's friend, Gertrude and suggested getting the four of us together.

Before that could happen, it was Ruthie, my Togenberg goat, our class mascot, which we kept in the shed next to the school, who changed everything. Ruthie gave birth to twins.

Now I had an excuse (ostensibly a reason) to phone Louella.

"Louella, it's Mark Green. Remember my class—from The Lab School? We visited last week? At the Trailside Museum? Well, our pet Togenberg goat, Ruthie, just gave birth. Two kids, a male and a female."

"Exciting!" she said. "Yes, of course I remember you."

"Yes, I said, "but here's the thing. I'm worried. I'm not sure if they are nursing. Could you come out to the school this evening and see how they're doing?" "No, I haven't seen either of them try to nurse."

"Glad to come," she said, "I'll bring a baby bottle from Trailside, just in case."

That evening she drove to the school in her little Volkswagen Beetle. I waited for her in the unlit parking lot.

"Here I am, Louella. Thanks for coming. Here, take my hand. We'll go out back to Ruthie's shed."

I felt for the light fixture dangling overhead at the end of an orange extension cord and switched it on. Ruthie stood to greet us. The two kids, lying on the straw, raised their heads, regarded us indifferently, and then let their heads flop down, back into the straw. I picked up the larger of the two, the male, and brought him to one of Ruthie's milk-engorged teats, but Ruthie stamped her hind legs and backed away.

"Here, Louella. I'll hold Ruthie steady. You see if you can get the baby to nurse."

Louella held one of the kids up to Ruthie's teat.

Nothing happened. Ruthie struggled in my grasp and the kid wouldn't suckle.

"OK, we'll try something different. Louella, you hold Ruthie by her collar. I'll milk her a bit, and we'll see if we can bottle feed them."

I squeezed out a cup-full of milk and poured it into the baby bottle Louella had brought.

We sat together on the straw-covered floor, encouraging the kids to suck from the bottle. It felt wonderful to be sitting there with Louella, our legs touching, our hands working together, stimulating the babies' cheeks to encourage the sucking reflex. They each took a few swallows of warm milk, neither drank with any enthusiasm.

"I'll come back tomorrow after work and see how they're doing," she said, standing up and brushing hay off her clothes.

"I appreciate your coming. Thanks." I held the door of Louella's Volkswagen as she lowered herself into the driver's seat. I bent down and kissed her lightly on the cheek.

But there was no need for her to return. By morning both kids were dead.

Our class held a funeral and burial in a field beside the school. Some of the children seemed upset. Some cried. I was disappointed and sad, but not devastated.

Ruthie, oblivious to the loss of her twins, appeared fine. She was now an important part of our curriculum: milking her twice a day, weighing and recording her daily production, pasteurizing the milk and converting it into cheese that we then sold.

Louella couldn't attend the funeral. She was at work. But she was very much on my mind and I was eager to see her again.

CHAPTER TWO

WE BEGAN to spend time together, Louella and I.

Once her friend Gertrude Barry became aware that Louella and I were a couple she invited me and my roommate, Jim, to her tiny apartment for a spaghetti dinner: a double date. Gertrude, like Louella, was a graduate of the college and was now completing a course in Swedish Massage.

When Jim and I arrived Gertrude was busy, squeezed into her tiny kitchen fussing with an elaborate meat sauce. Louella was setting the table.

We four soon settled in the living room where Gertrude served us pretzels and red wine. She poured it out of one of those cute bottles, wrapped in webbing and destined, when empty, to become a candle holder.

When we moved to the table Gertrude brought out a large bowl of spaghetti and meat sauce.

"I love your gravy" Jim said. I know you call it meat sauce, but in The Bronx, where I grew up, it was always just "Gravy.""

"Good, Jim. you call it what you want, but eat some more," Gertrude insisted. "I'm going to have more. I know I shouldn't but, Jim, you always tell me you like big bodied women. Right?"

"I do, I do." Jim agreed as Gertrude piled her plate high with a second serving.

Louella, who had already put down her utensils and neatly folded her cloth napkin, turned to Gertrude and suggested, "Tell the boys about Victor Lamotta."

"Oh," she said between mouthfuls, "He's something special. He's my spiritual teacher, Victor Lamotta. He's really transformed my life."

"How?" I asked.

"I feel so much better about myself. He teaches us the lessons he learned from the mystic, Gurdjief. Not from Gurjief himself, he's dead. From his books. He has us meditating and becoming self-aware. You really should come to our meetings. We call it "The Quest." We meet at the College library, Wednesday nights. Come. You'll see. It'll be good for you."

I heard her but suspected that anyone who consumed so much spaghetti still had a way to go in terms of self-awareness, let alone transformation.

The following Wednesday I asked Louella to have dinner with me in the town's best restaurant—the only one that used tablecloths. "I can't," she said. "I'm going to The Quest, that meeting Gertrude told us about. You come too."

I agreed, intrigued but skeptical.

It was a warm evening. The late setting June sun still brightened the library conference room. Fourteen of us sat on wooden folding chairs facing Victor Lamotta, the leader.

Silence. Victor sat still, hands on his knees, apparently composing himself. He was a slender man, of average height, perhaps, I judged, in his early forties. He smiled and looked at each of us in turn. Then he began to speak of the need to be present, to wake up. He said, "I'm sure you all remember an 'ah-hah' experience you've had that remains clearly etched in your mind, so clear that you can even see the colors and smell the smells—right? Those were the moments when you were truly awake. Wouldn't it be nice if, instead of having a few such minutes in your life you were able to string those moments together and be awake all the time?"

He elaborated on this theme and then we began to meditate.

Victor's guided meditation started out with a recollection of the body.

"Feel your weight pressing you into your chair," he intoned. "Feel your feet touching the floor. Be aware of sounds you are hearing, of smells you may be smelling, of taste if there be any." He went on for a minute or two and then abandoned us to silence and to self awareness.

I snuck a peek at my watch. *Fifteen minutes? Already?* I marveled at my ability to sit still so long, not to scratch my nose, not to change my position.

But I was hardly able to clear my mind. I couldn't just, "Let go of all thoughts," as Victor instructed. As I saw my attention wandering off. I recalled hearing once that it is impossible to stand in a corner for twenty minutes without thinking of a white polar bear. *It can't be done, you know. Try it. Stand in the corner of a room, facing the wall, for twenty minutes without once thinking of a white polar bear. No way.* The imaginary conversation took place in my mind and the realization that my thoughts were wandering brought a smile to my lips.

The act of smiling reminded me to take cognizance of my body and of my breath. I began to count inhalations.

On the second inhalation I wondered if my lesson plan for tomorrow was complete. From there my thoughts wandered to that unforgettable afternoon, a year ago, when things reached rock bottom for me. I saw myself, in my second month of teaching.—

Hallelujah, This school day is finished. But I won't dismiss them until they settle down and sit quietly. I refuse. I'm not going to give in and send them home. Not until they quiet down.

I turn to the IBM Selectric typewriter, behind my desk, my back to the class, and start composing a worksheet for tomorrow. The noise level rises. Soon paper airplanes fly across the classroom. Whack! One bumps my head and settles atop the typewriter.

I can't control these faculty brats. I'm finished. On the other hand, surely it can only get better from here on. I'm giving up—for now. Tomorrow will be a fresh start. I'm sure it can't get any worse.

I stand up, about to send them home. The words forming on my lips: "Get out of here!" *when -*

"Blangggg" My reverie was interrupted by the clash of two, small brass cymbals which Victor Lamotta held in his hands. The sound reverberated, diminished, and faded away.

The meditation was over.

Victor unfolded his lanky frame from his chair and slowly stood. With two hands he brushed his thinning hair, rearranging the long strands on the sides of his head to conceal the baldness on top. The rest of us stood, folded our chairs and began to put them away.

"Stop!" Victor called out. We all froze in place. "Work with attention. You should be able to put your chair away without making a sound. Now go ahead, and do it better this time."

We tried.

Victor approached Gertrude, Louella and me. "Thank you, Gertrude for bringing two guests." he said. "This is the Louella of whom you've spoken? Yes? I'm happy that you've joined The Quest, Louella. I hope to see more of you. And you, young fellow, how did you find the experience?"

I mumbled something polite but indistinct.

"If you stay with us we'll teach you to speak up clearly," he said smiling pleasantly and then turned to another of his students.

CHAPTER THREE

LOUELLA AND I parted from Gertrude, crossed to the parking lot and got into my eleven year old '49 Buick. We passed Main Street, where the town's single traffic light had already gone into "blinker" mode for the night and in three minutes we were at Louella's place.

Her second story efficiency apartment was in the home of the chairman of the mathematics department. Two years earlier he had hired Louella as a teaching assistant. The professor's wife, Louella's landlady, made it clear that at night male visitors were not permitted, so I understood that we mustn't speak as we climbed the narrow stairway in silence, Louella leading the way. I admired her shapely legs. She may be flat-chested, I thought, but her legs are exciting!

We were greeted by Louella's neutered gray tomcat. He had a name, but since I had little interest in cats, I refused to address it by name. We sat, side by side on the couch and I put my arm around Louella, which was the cat's signal to parade along the back of the couch and then snuggle into his mistress's lap.

Twice, I removed the cat from the couch. Finally Louella got up and prepared a treat for the animal.

"Here Sam, eat!" she said, putting his food down on the kitchen floor.

Then we were free to hug one another, to kiss, to stretch out fully along the couch; bodies pressed one to the other, each of us becoming increasingly excited.

Half an hour later I sat up and said "It's time I went home. We're both working tomorrow. I'll see you in the afternoon."

I had accepted her insistence that she was saving her virginity for the man she would someday marry, but it mystified me. *She's a year older than I am; twenty-four. When we cuddle and stroke each other she enjoys it as much as I do. Why does she deny herself the rest of it?*

At the door we kissed again and as I stepped out, onto the landing at the top of the stairway, Louella whispered, "Wait, we've hardly talked about the group." I stepped back inside and she continued in a normal voice, "You enjoyed the meditation, didn't you? Isn't Victor a good teacher? Are you going to come back with me next week?"

"Interesting. It was interesting. We'll see about next week. I'm not ready to make any promises."

For the next three weeks the spring weather was glorious. Maple trees came into full leaf. Alongside the roadways wild strawberries were ripe for picking. On each of those three Wednesday evenings I accompanied Louella, listened to Victor's teachings, and silently meditated for twenty minutes.

On the third of those evenings we walked across town rather than drive.

"OK," I said. "I know why you went there in the first place. You went because of your friend Gertrude. She was miserable and you say her life has been turned around. Great! But I'm not miserable. In fact, I'm relatively happy: happy being with you, and happy in my job. Well, nearly. I'm getting there, I think. What about you? You seem happy. Aren't you? So why do we keep going back?"

"You heard what Victor said. He says it again and again. "Try it. Don't take anything on faith. Pay attention and believe only what you see."

"What about the part where he said not to express negative emotions? I've always believed that if you bottle up your emotions and keep them to yourself you're asking for trouble."

"Don't make such a mystery out of it," Louella answered. "You've got to admit it's a great group of people—most of them. Relax and let it happen."

"Okay," I consented. "For you. But tell me when you think I've become enlightened. So far, I can't feel anything different happening."

*

Summer vacations came. Jim, my roommate, was graduated and found a job in Cleveland. Louella remained to teach mathematics in summer session and I went east, first to visit with my parents in New York City, then, back to the children's camp in Vermont where I had summered for so many years. I first went as a camper, then as a worker, and now I was head councilor and program director.

Camp had become a second home. Grace and Manny Gold, the owners, introduced me to a wholly different world, not the intellectual world of Manhattan's West Side, but the physical world of rural Vermont. Camp was their year-round home. They worked at farming the property, but their real "cash crop" was the summer campers. Their door was always open to me. Manny and I built bunkhouses. We worked together weeding rows of tomatoes and zucchini. When the toilets clogged we dug up the lawn and refurbished the stone-covered trench which country folk called "a blind drain."

Those were the things I did in my free time. Mostly. I devised program and made sure the campers were either happily occupied or asleep.

It was all the years of camp that led me to become a teacher, to find my first job at Horace Mann College, and there to meet Louella, to whom I managed to write letters nearly every day of our summer separation. Each night I wrote of the day's activities, of my worries— *Am I doing the right things? What will we do next? How will I figure out enough program to fill up the next seven weeks?*

"In truth," I wrote, "Louella, I do miss you, very much, but I'm so involved in my work. You'll have to forgive me for being so self-centered. I love you Louella. It's easy enough to write that, but my head is so full of camp, the job presses so hard on me, that I hardly remember what loving you means. Take care of yourself, and wait for me. Soon we'll be together again."

I left out any reference to the knot in my stomach or to the fact that I was constantly ticking off the days as they passed in descending order, towards the successful end of the season and to deliverance from the anxiety of failure.

Louella wrote to me just as often.

"It sounds as though I'm missing you more than you're missing me. That's okay. Do your work. Get a hold on yourself. We both know you can do it, and it isn't that many days before we'll be in each other's arms again. I love you.

Lou"

Eight weeks, fifty six days, each one noted to be aa day closer to the end of the season, and then camp was over. The children left and I remained another three days to help Manny close up.

"This morning," Manny said, "we'll butcher the sheep, before he becomes mutton." We'd never named him because of Manny's policy not to name any animal they intended to eat.

Manny gathered his butchering implements. I went to the animal's pen in the barn. The cute lamb had morphed into a smelly, randy beast. As I struggled to push a stout rope through his leather collar he kept climbing my leg, wrapping his forelegs around my body, trying to mount me. Finally, with difficulty, clumsily, I tugged the protesting beast into the barnyard, over to where Manny stood with his twenty-two caliber rifle.

Manny loaded the gun and tried to hold it to the ram's head. Easier said than done. The intended victim greeted the proffered rifle by embracing the barrel, encircling it with his forelegs, and mounting the rifle with the same enthusiasm and passion he would have offered to any available ewe.

Then, with a scarcely audible crack from the rifle it was all over: my first experience with unbridled, uncontrolled masculine lust.

Early the next morning I left Vermont, drove into the evening, then through the night. By nine in the morning I arrived at Louella's apartment in Cold Springs, Ohio. I parked and rang the buzzer at the foot of the stairs. She bounded down. We embraced, kissed, and she pulled me into the landing.

"You're here at last!" she said. "I'm so happy! Let me look at you." She held my hands while kicking the door shut.

"Shhhh," I whispered. "Aren't we supposed to be quiet here?"

"Who cares," she said. You're back," and she led me up the narrow flight of stairs.

Being with Louella felt so right; as though I had never been away.

Two days later the new term began. My third year of teaching. It was good to be teaching again, as if I'd never left. But with Jim gone my bungalow felt empty—not when Louella visited, but otherwise. I missed the assurance of sharing my life with someone.

Three weeks into the term, on a crisp October afternoon, Louella came to my place, as she often did. Wearing sweaters, we sat outside, sipping beer and noting the leaves, just offering a hint of the changes already begun. After a while she left me outdoors, and went inside to prepare supper. We ate. Then, while I washed the dishes, she ensconced herself onto the living room couch, and spread stacks of exam papers over the coffee table.

"Why don't you grade them the traditional way?" I suggested from the kitchen.

"What's that?"

"You know. Take them to your place. Drop them down the stairs. The ones on the top steps get an "A", lower ones, a "B," and the very bottom are all "Fs.'"

"Hah! Some joke. You can grade your papers any way you want. I'm a departmental assistant, remember? These aren't from my class. I get to do everyone else's scut work."

I put down the dishtowel and snuggled beside her.

"You poor overworked dear," I said, putting my arms around her.

"Stop," she said. "I'm working."

I didn't stop and soon we were horizontal on the couch—shoes removed—the lights off. We explored each other's bodies. My hands found the slickness between her legs. She unbuckled my belt, my pants, unzipped my fly.

All too soon, "No more," Louella cautioned me.

"Why? Why no more, Louella? It's so good!"

"You know why. That's for the man I'll marry. Only when I'm married."

I held her tightly, my hands no longer under her clothing.

"All right. Let's get married."

Louella untangled her body from mine and put her feet to the floor. She stared down, into my face for what seemed like an inappropriately long time, then smiled and said, "Yes! Really? Yes! Let's do it. Christmas vacations. In New York. With our families."

After Louella gathered her exam papers and drove home, My thoughts turned to the ram that Manny and I had slaughtered, just a few weeks ago. *I'm just like that ram, aren't I? Clearly, Louella won't sleep with me until I marry her. Am I ready for that? Yes. I think so. She's my kind of person. I can live with her, happily, for the rest of my life. Sure I can. Christmas is only a couple of months away.*

CHAPTER FOUR

I'D HAD barely, a few days to adjust to the idea of impending marriage when, at the end of one school day, a large form appeared, practically obscuring the classroom door. It was Dr. Thomas Lacy. Even though many of my students knew him, they hastened to stand aside and make way as he strode into the room.

I knew Dr. Lacy, from the gym. though not well, A group of faculty members gathered two afternoons a week for volleyball. Sometimes I joined in. Lacy was always there. Aside from having a massive build, he possessed an intimidating and overpowering volleyball serve. Tom Lacy was also Chairman of the Psychology Department. And he was the father of Bobby Lacy, the one, of all my ten year old boys, who most resembled Huckleberry Finn.

Dr. Lacy stood by my desk, waiting until we were alone. Then, with one hand he seized the nearest desk-and-chair combination, effortlessly pulled it up to my desk, and perched atop the unit.

"Listen," he growled. "Mr. Green—Mark—My son Bobby is ten years old. There's nothing the matter with him. But he never picks up a book. It's time for him to start reading books. Don't tell me about reading readiness. I know all of that psychology. I'm head of the damned Psych Department for God's sake, and I don't give a rat's ass. There's nothing wrong with my boy. I want to see him reading by the end of this year. I want you to make it happen. This year, not next year."

It was a short, one-sided conversation. Dr. Lacy wasn't asking me what I thought. He was telling me what he expected of me. At least I got the recognition of hearing him mutter, on the way out, "See you in the gym."

*

Louella and I were not living together—and wouldn't be, until our December wedding. But she had largely taken over the kitchen in my bungalow, which would soon be hers. That night, over dinner, I repeated most of Lacy's tirade.

"Terrible, Mark. It makes me angry, just listening. How did it make you feel?"

"I'm not sure. It left me with a churning in my stomach. But that's nothing new. It happens whenever I'm stumped, when I don't know what I should be teaching. I haven't the vaguest idea how I'm going to turn Bobby into a reader. He isn't interested. And, yes, that man scares me. He scares me when we play volleyball, and now I'm scared for my job. No way they'll ask me back for another year if Lacy is against me."

Louella thought for a moment. She put down her knife and fork, folded her paper napkin and placed it on the table. She looked at me with full attention.

"You know what I think, Mark? We both need to go back to The Quest, to Victor Lamotta's group. Every time I see Gertrude she talks about how much better she feels. She doesn't let things bother her. You can tell, she's got more perspective on life. Give it another try. I think it will help you."

"Maybe."

"Not 'maybe.' We'll do it together. You can't go through life with your insides churning. You need this."

"Well—okay—for a while. At five bucks a session. What's to lose?"

CHAPTER FIVE

THE QUEST had prospered during my summer absence. No longer meeting in the college library, now Victor leased the unused church annex, an ancient wooden structure at the edge of town, abandoned by the congregation when they built newer quarters.

Louella and I were a few minutes late. As we entered. The musty smell of decaying wood brought me back to Camp, to the Vermont farmhouse that I knew so well. Many of the people, already seated, were familiar, but membership had grown, and at least half the faces were new. Some twenty participants already waited in silent anticipation, their chairs in rows, facing a larger, wooden chair on which Victor normally sat. I was pleased to see Gertrude sitting there. She rose, came and embraced Louella. Gertrude beamed; she possessed a presence which I had never seen before.

"I'm so glad you have rejoined us. Sit down and we'll talk right after the meeting."

She kissed me on the cheek and then returned to her chair, facing the group.

"Victor will be late tonight," she announced. I sensed a silent wave of discontent. Or perhaps it was just my own disappointment. "I'll bring us through the awareness exercise and the meditation, then if he gets here, he will do the lesson."

Taking Victor's accustomed place, facing the group, Gertrude led us in a chant. Then she repeated Victor's standard instructions. "Sense the parts of your body, be aware that you are the one who is sensing. Let idle thoughts pass by without carrying you away. Notice the thought you are entertaining and just let it go."

Then came twenty minutes of meditation.

Instead of thinking about nothing, I found myself speculating.

Why is Gertrude leading the group? Why not Victor? What does she mean "if he gets here"? She's doing a decent job of filling in. She doesn't seem nervous, being alone up there. I certainly would be!

The abrupt clash of miniature cymbals jerked me out of my meditation and there, seated, facing us, was Victor, his eyes and the corners of his lips in a self-satisfied grin. He peered from face to face, acknowledging everyone's presence, and then began.

"Tonight's topic is awareness—about the importance of paying attention to the job at hand, be it composing a symphony or scrubbing a floor." He went on, introducing us to the concept of "the working surface."

"Whatever you are doing, that is where you must keep your attention," he said.

"When you're driving your car, the working surface is where the tires meet the road. That's where your attention belongs. Not listening to the radio."

It took ten minutes for Victor to flesh out the concept.

He concluded by announcing, "On Sunday we will have a work day, right here, in the annex. You should arrive at eight in the morning and bring a lunch with you."

Oi, I thought. *My precious Sunday morning! Eight o'clock! Well, this is the way it goes. 'In for a nickel, in for a dollar.' or whatever the saying is.*

CHAPTER SIX

TWENTY MINUTES before the alarm was set to ring I woke to the sharp staccato of sleet drumming against my window; the first storm of the coming winter.

Am I really going out in this weather? Insanity. But I did promise Louella I'd go, even though she can't make it. "Show the flag" sort of. What the hell.

I rose and prepared for the "work day," which I'd be attending without Louella. Her plans included going to church in the morning and spending the rest of the day in her own warm apartment correcting math papers.

I parked my old Buick in the lot, behind the annex, got out of the car and pulled the hood of my ski jacket tightly around my head, fending off the driving sleet.

Once I got inside, it was still cold, but at least the building was wind-tight. In the dim light, I was pleased to see that twelve of us had shown up to work. I read the placard hung from the raised stage at the far end of the hall. "Wake Up!" was scrawled in a child's handwriting. The letters diminished in size as they covered the sheet of brown wrapping paper.

I recognized one of my fellow volleyball players, Al Kramer. Al was in the Geology Department. In fact, he was the whole geology department. He was a large, teddy bear of a fellow, the long hair on his head merging into his bushy beard.

"Hey," I said. "I didn't know you were a member of The Quest. That's what I get for having been away all summer."

"Then welcome back," he said, enveloping me in his massive arms.

"Good to see you too, Al. Yes. For better or for worse, I'm here now, not really committed. Still trying it out."

Our conversation was interrupted by a piercing whistle, the kind you make by putting two fingers, one from each hand, into the corners of your mouth and blowing hard: a skill I'd never been able to master. It came from Jeremy O'hara, a long-time member whose assignment today was "work supervisor." Instant quiet. *A surprise, I* thought, *such obedience demanded and received by such a mild mannered man.*

Jeremy proceeded to assign jobs. Al Kramer and I, along with two others, were to sandpaper the wooden floor—to bring it to a smooth luster. We were each given a chunk of two-by-four, about two hand's width in length, which we wrapped with sheets of sandpaper. We'd be working on our knees. "Remember," Jeremy reminded us, "work with attention. The whole point is to keep your full attention on the working surface, the place where the sandpaper meets the floor."

Al knew the two women we'd be working with. "Meet Hannah Mays," he said, introducing me to the older of the two, whose tight, curly hair was more white than black.

"Pleased to meet you," she said, firmly shaking my hand. "Indeed. I've seen you around town," she said in a distinctly German accent. "Now I know who you are."

She looked me straight in the eye and I sensed she had no room for frivolity or small talk.

"And this is Laura Steiner," Al said. "She was one of my star pupils last year in beginning geology, you know—rocks for jocks."

"Hi," said the tall, dark-haired college student, smiling, shaking her head and tossing her long hair over her shoulders. "I'm not a jock though. I'm in the theatre department, and majoring in speech."

"Hi," I answered. "That sounds like a lot of work."

"Not so bad," she said with a wink.

The four of us knelt down, and started off in a line: Al, me, Hannah on my right and Laura on the end.

Laura's white blouse was loosely tied in front by a white cord.

When we got down onto our knees the blouse hung open, revealing her ample breasts, even the prominent nipples, unfettered by a brassiere. The sight both excited me and upset me. *How am I supposed to react? Am I supposed to ignore the sight? Pretend I'm not interested? There is a sexual revolution going on that I've completely missed, isn't there? I can pretend I'm not looking—just peek once in awhile. No way can I tell myself that I'm paying more attention to the working surface, where the sandpaper meets the floor, than I am to the sight of Laura Steiner's breasts, swaying enticingly as she rhythmically strokes the floor boards.*

We worked in silence. Periodically I looked around to see how the others were doing. Soon, we were no longer in a line. Al had pulled several feet ahead, and the college girl, Laura Steiner, was behind me. Hannah Mays and I were still side by side.

Mostly, when I looked back it was to peer down the dark-haired girl's blouse. But right after each peek I was able to pull myself together and remember Victor's words; "Pay attention. It isn't how fast you complete the job. It doesn't even matter whether you finish or don't finish. What's important is that you work with attention."

Again, my attention strayed, this time to Hannah's forearm, where the blue tattoo was clearly visible—A104603.

It wasn't the first time I had seen such tattoos. On Manhattan's West Side, where I'd grown up, survivors of Hitler's camps were numerous. But not here in the countryside of Ohio. The horrors that Hannah had obviously gone through were not something I wanted to think about. I simply filed away the tattoo's existence and refused to dwell on its implications. Instead, I glanced backward to take another look down Laura's blouse. Laura caught my glance, met it, and kept on with her back and forth sanding of the floor. Embarrassed at having been caught, I spun my head around and furiously attacked the wooden floorboards ahead of me.

Peripherally, I became aware of a figure at the table across the room, pouring something into cups.

It was Victor Lamotta who had emerged from the back office where he sometimes held individual conferences. "Time for a break," he called out. "Come. Take a drink and rest for a moment, then we'll get back to work."

The paper cups contained cold water.

"Drink with attention. As you drink, be aware of each of your senses," Victor intoned. "Know that you are drinking. Know that it is you who is drinking."

Al Kramer, standing next to me, sipped from his cup, bent his bushy face toward me, grinned and whispered, "I'm getting a buzz already."

We worked attentively for another two hours. It was two in the afternoon when someone said "Time to stop now." by which time the pain in my knees was excruciating. It was Gertrude who said, "Time to stop now."

Victor apparently was elsewhere.

By now the pain in my knees was terrible. Al had to help me up from the floor.

On our way home, Al and I stopped at a roadside bar for something stronger than Victor's water. Over our mugs of beer, I asked him, "You've been around this longer than I have. Tell me where Victor got all this stuff."

"You mean 'wisdom' don't you? Here's how it was explained to me," Al said. "Years ago, Victor belonged to a group in New York City, followers of the Middle-Eastern mystic, Gurdjief. I've heard they kicked him out because he wouldn't accept some assignment they gave him. No idea what the assignment was, but he didn't like it. Anyway, he left them. He and his wife, and their two little boys, moved out here to Ohio and he set up his own group. He wanted to put his own stamp on the material so he called it 'The Quest.' That's his own name for the teachings he'd brought along. Kind of his own brand. He's a maverick, I'd say, but a wonderful teacher. And the ideas he's spreading, they seem to be true—life changing—how to live your life properly."

"Hmmmm. Okay. Now tell me about our two partners, you seem to know them pretty well. Tell me about Hannah and Laura."

"Well, first off, I wouldn't call her Hannah, at least not till you know her much better. Mrs. Mays is kind of old school. Her husband is head of the Physics department. Good man."

"Okay. I won't make that mistake again. What about Laura?"

Al looked into my eyes a moment, winked, and then said, "Don't be getting ideas Mark, you're about to be married. Keep it zipped up till then."

I finished my beer without responding to Al's challenge.

CHAPTER SEVEN

CHRISTMAS HOLIDAYS. Our wedding date arrived. We gathered at Louella's childhood home, a three-story detached Victorian in Queens where we would be married in the parlor. Jim, my ex-roommate, flew from Cleveland to be best man. He came in his one and only suit, an aging, brown outfit that appeared scruffy in contrast to my newly purchased dark-blue suit.

Gertrude, his erstwhile girlfriend, was maid of honor. She wore a pink dress that Louella had designed. Louella had even found and purchased the fabric, but Gertrude had sewn the dress. It didn't try to hide her heft. Instead, it showed off each of her extra pounds to an attractive advantage. I was pleased to see Gertrude looking so buoyant and at home in her body. Louella, in a gown we brought from Cold Springs, was radiant! Her blue eyes sparkled. Her calm self-assurance fully compensated for my nervousness. Grace and Manny drove down from their farm-camp in Vermont. Louella's sister was there with her young daughter and our two sets of parents completed the wedding party.

First chance he got to have me alone, Jim pulled me by the sleeve, into the parlor, a small room, where two overstuffed chairs faced a newly acquired ten inch television set, housed in an ornate wooden cabinet.

"Sit," he said. I need to talk to you. It's about Gertrude."

"Sure. What's the big bru-ha-ha?"

"I'm going crazy," he said. "She's so wrapped up in this damn spiritual thing–The Quest–she doesn't seem to think about anything else. She hardly answers my letters. She doesn't want to talk on the phone. What is it, Mark? It's a cult. Isn't it?"

"No," I said. I don't think it's a cult. Louella and I still go to it. What keeps it from being a cult, maybe, is that Victor, keeps telling us not to take his word for any of it, to try it out and see for ourselves. It seems, to me that he's got ahold of something good—ancient wisdom stuff, pretty profound truths. At first it seems to be way out stuff. But the longer you live with it, the truer it all seems."

Before Jim could respond Mr. Cook came to the door and said, "Someone in a dark suit is here and asking for you, Mark. He may be the preacher. He's nobody I've seen before."

My mother had arranged for Dr. Springer, of the Ethical Cultural Society to officiate. "No charge," he'd explained in the German accent of a recent war refugee. "I specialize in the performance of mixed marriages. It is a service which our Society offers." The slender minister with dark hair and a narrow black mustache introduced himself to me. I, in turn, called upstairs to Louella, who came right down.

Dr Springer, taking charge, beckoned the two of us to follow him into the empty kitchen where we three sat to confer.

"Tell me," he said, "is there anything special that you would like me to include in the ceremony?"

"Yes," I answered, "I'd like to include the Jewish ritual of the breaking of a wine glass—stomping on it."

"You can do that," he answered, "but then I won't be able to perform the ceremony. Breaking the glass symbolizes rupturing of the hymen. It represents man's domination over woman. I won't participate in that barbaric ritual."

That differed from my interpretation. I'd always thought it symbolized the destruction of the temple. "*Let me remember you, Jerusalem, at the height of my happiness,*" is written in the Psalms. So we left it out.

The ceremony was brief. Louella and I stood, in front of the fireplace, facing Dr. Springer—family and friends behind us. My legs trembled the whole time. When Dr. Springer asked me, "Do you promise to love, honor, cherish and protect Louella, forsaking all others forevermore." I experienced a momentary questioning, but, with no obvious hesitation, said, "I do."

Once Dr. Springer took his leave and drove off, Louella and I went outside, where Jim photographed me as I stomped down, crushing a tumbler wrapped in a linen napkin.

Then we all drove to Manhattan where, at The Tavern On The Green a small, private dining room awaited us. Gertrude and Jim, sat together and offered several toasts, each trying to outdo the other in predicting a bright future for us newlyweds.

Jim stood and clanged his fork on his wine glass, demanding silence. He raised his glass and said, "This time, it won't be another toast to the bride and groom. This one is to the bridesmaid, Gertrude, and the best man. That's me—the best man. Congratulations to the two of us for our great accomplishment in bringing this pair together. Remember, Gertrude and I knew each other before Mark and Louella ever met. What a thrill it was, playing matchmaker—and what a marvelous result! Raise your glasses again. A toast to the matchmakers. And what's more...."

I watched Gertrude. Her lips were tightly pursed. She reached out for her wineglass, caught her sleeve on the cutlery in front of her, jerked her arm back, and in doing so, upset her full glass of dark-red Merlot. The ensuing commotion drowned out the rest of Jim's toast. Disappointed, he sat down while Louella and her sister snatched up all the napkins within their reach and blotted the table. Louella took her water glass in hand and dabbed at the wine stains on Gertrude's dress.

Mr. Cook turned to my father. "So, what did you think of the game last night! That was something, huh!"

"What game?" my father answered. "I'm not really a sports fan."

Mr. Cook tried again. "How about fishing? Do you fish? We've got some wonderful fishing out at our summer place on the tip of Long Island. We should try it together some time."

"We'll see," my father replied.

I proposed a toast of my own: "To Gertrude and Jim. Thank you both for your friendship and support. If our marriage served no other purpose than to bring you two together again it would have been worthwhile!"

Everybody clapped as Jim leaned to kiss Gertrude. The kiss had been directed at her lips but Gertrude turned away and it only reached her cheek.

We spent our wedding night and the remaining three days of our vacation in my parents' apartment in Manhattan which they vacated for us by going up to their country place in Westchester County.

That night, in my parents' guest room, was the long deferred consummation. It wasn't the earth-rocking departure I had so long anticipated—we still had a lot to learn about pleasuring one another, but I fell asleep happily secure in the knowledge that we now belonged to each other, fully.

CHAPTER EIGHT

FOUR DAYS later we returned to Ohio and Louella moved her possessions into my cottage. I cut a small passage into the back door so that Sam could attend to his cat business without unduly bothering me.

In the spring quarter the Math Department gave Louella a section of her own to teach. My teaching was becoming more comfortable—relatively speaking. I still approached each morning with the same knot in my stomach, with the same fear that I wouldn't know how to fill up the day, that I would run out of things for the children to do.

As warm weather approached my class went through crazes. The girls played jacks every free moment. The boy's read Captain Marvel Comics; Captain Marvel and only Captain Marvel. Not any other comics. Even Bobby Lacy was reading them. He still wasn't reading books, but he did read those comics.

Then the boys brought water guns to school. Entering or leaving the building meant passing through a moist torrent. That afternoon, during a silent time, the children were writing stories and I was at my desk. In the back of the room Billy Hollister stood up with a pistol in each hand. He aimed and he shot at his younger cousin Joan.

"Oh, no, William. Never." I said. "Give me those pistols. I'll take them home for safekeeping until you learn to control yourself in class."

The school-day concluded in peace. About an hour after school I was in our kitchen when Louella called out from the bedroom,

"Mark, I hear voices." Then someone knocked on the back door. I opened.

"Hands up, Mister Green!" I hesitated and three strands of water splashed directly into my face.

"Got you, Mister Green!"

I slammed the door. Louella came down the hall to see what was happening. Smiling, I put a finger to my lips. "Sheeh" I gestured that she follow me to the bedroom. I rummaged in my dresser and found the confiscated water guns. We quickly filled them from the bathroom sink. Louella and I went out the front door, snuck around to the back and ambushed the three intruders.

"Wham. Now you're dead Bobby Lacy, Neal Brodsky and Sean O'Connor."

"No we aren't. I'm only wounded," said Bobby, firing back at us.

We ran back in the direction from which we had come and ducked behind a hedge. The three of them chased us, found our hiding place and began firing.

"Surrender, Mr. Green. You too, Louella!"

"You're outnumbered, Mr. Green. You'd better give up!"

We did. We gave up, and invited the three boys into the house for cold drinks. I returned the confiscated water guns. "But don't you dare bring them back to school," I warned. The boys stayed with us for a few minutes, not once firing their guns inside the house. Then they left to continue their gun play elsewhere.

"That was fun," said Louella. "I really like the way you are with your kids these days."

"Thanks. But did you notice the main thing? I'm 'Mr. Green' to them because that's the way the administration wants me to be addressed. They say it makes for more respect. Hah! I've never had anybody shoot a water gun at me before while addressing me as 'Mr. Green!'"

Within a week the water guns disappeared. Similarly, the interest in Captain Marvel evaporated. A few of the boys turned their attention toward our classroom shelf of Sherlock Holmes mysteries.

Bobby Lacy picked one up, was enchanted, and didn't stop reading for the rest of the term.

On the final day of school, coming for his son, Dr. Lacy took me aside and said, "I don't know how to thank you, Mark. You did what I asked. You turned Bobby into a reader. Whatever you did, it worked and we are very pleased with you." The big man reached out, took my hand in his and shook it warmly; his powerful hands, so intimidating on the volleyball court, now conveyed affection and appreciation

I mumbled something modest. "It wasn't my doing at all. Bobby did it by himself." Lacy didn't believe me.

I watched the big man leave my classroom, my fingers still tingling from his handshake.

He's my friend now. Tom Lacey is on my side. What a relief!

CHAPTER NINE

LOUELLA AND I walked home from Victor's Wednesday evening talk. In a week we'd be off to Europe for our deferred honeymoon. We strolled, hand in hand, under the maples, foliage blotting out the last traces of twilight. We were silent, listening to the chorus of spring peepers, at times barely audible and then rising to a deafening crescendo

"So?" I asked, interrupting Louella's thoughts. "Did you get anything out of tonight's session?"

"Maybe. You tell me first. What do you think?"

"It's hard. I've still got no idea what meditation is supposed to be doing for me—to me—anything." More silence, then I said, "But his teachings make sense. And we're enjoying the people, aren't we? I think that's what keeps me coming back."

"Yes," she answered. "It seems this is the only place I see Gertrude any more. She's totally involved in The Quest. No doubt there. And you keep telling me how much you appreciate Hannah."

"Yeah. Not like when I first met her, that cold day in the annex, scraping the floor. You weren't there. I thought she was forbidding, kind of... Now she's our buddy, a pussy cat."

"She's not a pussy cat," Louella corrected me. "She's a grand old lady, and it's a privilege getting to know her."

"Yeah," I said.

"That's okay," Louella responded. "You don't make me jealous. Her husband, Dr. Otto Mays is a big man on campus. You're no threat to him."

"Thanks for the vote of confidence," I answered, putting my arm around her shoulder.

*

Two days day before we were to leave for Europe, Hannah and Otto Mays hosted a picnic for The Quest at their farm, a place we were coming to know well.

My goat, Ruthie, in the back seat, was going to spend the summer vacation in the Mays' barn. As we drove down the dirt lane Ruthie, standing uncomfortably on the floor between the front and back seats, perked up her head in excitement. She sensed the presence of other goats, as well as sheep, cattle and chickens. I parked in front of the immense, gambrel-roofed barn, opened the paddock gate, and then opened the rear door. Ruthie clumsily backed out from between the seats, then, turned loose, she scampered away in search of company.

"Have a wonderful summer," I called after her.

The picnic was well underway. Everybody was out behind the two-story, white clapboard farmhouse, on the flagstone patio. Dr. Mays, manning the grill, was serving hot dogs and hamburgers to order.

I spied Victor, standing by the beverage table. Next to him was a woman I took to be his wife, the mysterious person of whom we all knew but had never met. Victor caught my eye and beckoned to us.

"Come, meet my family. Now you'll finally get to meet Cora, my wife. Cora, this is Mark Green, one of my smarter students." Victor gave me a knowing wink and said, to his wife, "He shows some promise. He may develop into something, but I'm still not sure. And this is Louella," Victor said. "She's a real gem. Maybe more than Mark deserves, but too busy to come every week, or so she believes. Sometimes she comes to class. Sometimes not. You never can count on her."

Louella turned to Mrs.Lamotta, smiled and reached out to shake her hand. "We're so pleased, finally, to meet you, Cora. It's well over a year we've known you just as a disembodied name."

Cora met Louella's handshake, but without very much warmth.

"And your boys? Are your boys here," I asked.

Victor pointed toward the barbecue where his
teen-age boys were awaiting hamburgers.

"Paul, Vicky, come meet..."

His boys, oblivious to Victor's calls, took their food and disappeared toward the barn.

"Well, you'll meet them later."

Cora, whom we had all been curious to meet, was of dark complexion, medium height, not very talkative. We knew, from Victor that she was a public school nurse, working in a nearby town. This was the first time she had shown up for any of The Quest's functions and we observed her with interest which Cora didn't seem to reciprocate. She spent most of the afternoon exploring the farm on her own.

We had a single month in which to take in all that Europe could offer us, or as much as we were able to absorb in that short time. Our guidebook, you might say our bible, was *Europe on $5 a day*. Many of our nights were spent in youth hostels, but even on our limited budget the food we ate was astounding. Louella claimed that the highlight, for both of us, was a spectacular tureen of bouillabaisse which we shared in an outdoor restaurant on the Italian Riviera.

I might agree, but that afternoon I was equally captivated by the beauty of the sparkling blue Mediterranean, just in front of us, and by the crowd of sparrows that kept pestering us, begging for another morsel of food.

The weeks went by in a blur, and at the end of our time abroad we were quite ready to resume our lives in Cold Springs.

The afternoon we arrived back on campus our telephone rang. It was Hannah Mays. In her strong German accent she said, "I saw you driving through town. Welcome back. We need to talk. Come to our house. Tonight. I'll make you dinner."

"We'd love to come, Hannah. What are you so eager to talk about?"

"So you've heard nothing? Tonight then. Come at six thirty."—"No"—"Bring nothing, but prepare to be surprised."

So promptly at six thirty, driving down the farm lane, I slowed our Buick in front of the barn, intending to greet Ruthie.

"Not now," Louella insisted, "Hannah has something important to tell us. We'll see your goat afterwards, tomorrow, when we take her back."

Dr. Otto Mays greeted us at his door.

"Welcome. We're so glad you came. Come in. Sit down."

As close as I felt to Hannah, her husband intimidated me. I was in awe of his worldliness, his accomplishments, and his courtly manner. Dr. Mays' German accent was even more pronounced than his wife's. "Hannah is in the kitchen where I'm not allowed to bother her but the martinis are ready so, please, be seated."

We sat in high-backed chairs facing the fireplace where smoldering logs glowed red. Dr. Otto Mays stirred the embers with a poker and then added a fresh log which immediately burst into flame. On the coffee table were cheese, crackers and drinks. This would be my first martini, ever. *This is what sophisticated people drink.* I told myself. *It's time I learn to drink it.* I took a sip. *Awful, Ugh! But if this is what Dr. Mays likes, I'll learn to like it too. This must be what they mean by "an acquired taste."*

Coming from the kitchen and wiping her hands on a flowery apron, Hannah joined us before my glass was empty. The three of us stood up. Hannah kissed Louella and me.

"It feels like forever. Look at the two of you! You look so good. Was it wonderful? But why are we standing? Sit. Everybody."

We all sat, and Hannah continued, "Later. Later you will tell us all about your trip. Since you just got back you don't know yet, so I'll tell you what happened." Hannah paused, took a deep breath, blew it out, and said, "Victor's wife kicked him out of her house. He's living in the storeroom, upstairs in the annex."

"Holy Moly!" I said, repeating the words of my students' hero, Captain Marvel.

"Why?" Louella asked.

"First, a question," said Hannah. "You and Gertrude are very close, aren't you?"

"We used to be. Less so since Mark and I got married. She and Mark's roommate, Jim, used to be a couple. But since Jim moved away we rarely see her outside of The Quest."

"Well," Hannah continued, "it seems that Victor's wife suspected that something was going on. She hired a detective who hid a recording device in the back room at The Annex. Sure enough. Victor and Gertrude have been having assignations there, if that's what you call it. And as soon as she had the evidence, Victor's wife kicked him out of the house."

"Poor Gertrude must have been mortified to be discovered, exposed that way," Louella said. "Does everybody know about them?"

"Oh yes!"

"What about our group? How are they taking it?" I asked.

"Each in his or her own way," Hannah answered. "Al Kramer spoke up at the first meeting after word got out and he asked Victor, right out, 'Explain yourself' he said."

"And did he?" I asked.

"Of course he did," she answered. "And I believe I am quoting: 'The most important thing is The Quest. Everything is for the good of The Quest. Gertrude and I move it forward, This was meant to happen and it's not to be interfered with.'"

"Did anyone go for it?" I asked.

"As you may imagine, opinion is divided," Hannah answered stiffly.

"And you? What do you think?" I asked.

Now, for the first time since Hannah's revelation began, Otto Mays spoke up: "Let me, please, answer for both of us. Even though I am not a participant in the group, I can speak. We are both survivors of the war. Hannah returned from the camps. I was one of the lucky ones. I got out in time, before it was too late, but most of my family perished. We know there is right action and wrong action. We learned one important lesson. You do not excuse bad actions.

You do not excuse bad people. Therefore my wife will no longer be taught by this man. I wouldn't allow it. Nor would she choose it. But you two, you, of course, will make your own decisions."

We talked about many things through supper. Our host and hostess wanted to hear all our impressions of Europe, but Victor and Gertrude were never far from our thoughts. When coffee was served Louella asked, "Mrs. Mays...Hannah, there must be more to tell us? Do you know how their affair started?"

"Yes," Hannah answered. "I know at least part of the tale. It was just before Gertrude's final examination to become a certified and licensed masseuse. Victor invited her to stay after class, to practice for the exams. It started with a massage. I can just imagine the rest of it!"

A short silence followed her words. Dr. Mays, his arms crossed in front of him, looked fierce. Hannah was upset by the retelling of the story. Louella was obviously distressed. I did my best to resist Hannah's suggestion to "imagine the rest of it."

Instead, I promised to come back in the morning to retrieve Ruthie. Then I stood up, saying, "You'll have to excuse us, It's been a very long day Hannah and Dr. Mays. For us this day started in England, twenty hours ago."

On the ride home Louella said, "Gertrude is my friend. I need to talk to her. I won't condemn her. But Victor is a scum bag. How could he do that to his wife? If he loves Gertrude then he should have told his wife, not make her find out the terrible way she did."

CHAPTER TEN

LOUELLA PRESERVED her friendship with Gertrude but she was emphatically through with The Quest. "No more for me!" she said. "You can keep going to Victor's talks if you want to, but without me"

Since Victor's teachings were beginning to make sense to me, I continued with him. So did my friend Al. But fully half of the group saw it the way Hannah and Louella did and they disappeared from our meetings.

We no longer had The Quest to share with Hannah but, nevertheless, Louella and I found ourselves visiting the Mays with increasing frequency.

Hannah and Otto Mays were worldly, accomplished people. In no way could we think of ourselves as being on their level, but being left with no remaining family after the war, they now welcomed the two of us as family. Often, on weekends, I would assist Otto with some task that required more than two hands.

I loved communing with the sights and smells of their farm; the chickens, who had the run of the property, the goats, even the smell of their buck, Hugo, who once a year had the opportunity of coupling with my goat, Ruthie. Every time we visited the farm I felt myself transported back to my Vermont summer camp.

On one memorable occasion Otto came to my school and lectured my fifth and sixth graders about physics. Often rambunctious and unaccepting of strangers, they were entranced, completely under his spell as he described the world of physics in clear, understandable terms.

*

Victor announced a new work project. Unlike the time when we polished the Annex floor, back then it didn't matter if we finished or not, the whole point was to pay attention, this time it was all practical.

In just two weekends plus a couple of evenings of work, we insulated an upstairs section of the Annex, nailed up sheetrock, taped the joints, painted the walls and produced a bedroom into which Gertrude and Victor moved.

After one of those work parties I invited Al to come by my house for a beer.

Louella greeted him with a hug and a kiss.

"We don't see enough of you anymore, Al. I'm so glad you're here."

"You don't see me because you don't come to The Quest anymore, Louella. That's why."

"Mea Culpa," she answered. "Anyway, welcome to our home!"

Al and I took our beers into the living room and sat, he in the stuffed armchair and I on the couch. Louella remained in the kitchen.

I asked, "Do you want me to get you a towel or something, to pat your beard dry? I never could figure how you manage to strain drinks through that thing."

"Don't try to be smart, Mark. You're just jealous."

Our conversation went from bantering, to a discussion about various people in The Quest, then, inevitably, to talk about Victor.

"Al, We've had this talk before. Do you remember that cold day in the Annex when we scraped the floor and rubbed our knees raw? Back then I asked you about how Victor got here."

"Yeah. I remember"

"Well there's got to be more. What's the real reason they kicked him out of the movement? Do you know?"

"Maybe. Rumors, more than anything else. Wait a minute, first I need another beer."

Al disappeared into the kitchen, then returned with a fresh can of beer, sat, popped it open, and continued, "I told you, they had an organized structure there in Brooklyn and, apparently, Victor didn't fit into it very well. He had a tendency to do things his own way. But, according to one version, what really got them upset was when one of his students accused him of molesting her or something. It may have happened more than once.

"I suspected something like that," I said. "It fits. That's certainly the Victor we know."

"Yeah," Al said, "but don't be too hard on him. The stuff he's teaching us is pretty strong. I, for one, appreciate him. Nobody's all of a piece, are they?

New recruits were constantly finding their way to The Quest. Victor divided his students into two groups; those of us who had been around for a while, and the relative newcomers. One evening after class Victor called me over and asked, "Mark, how about you coming in tomorrow and leading the beginners class through a guided meditation? Then I'll teach the lesson."

"Sure. I'll be glad to."

Surprisingly, the next night I was less nervous about the prospects of leading this group than I usually feel about meeting with my own fifth and sixth graders. After all, I thought, if I run out of things to say, I'll just tell them to meditate in silence.

Eleven people sat facing me in two rows, five men and six women, ranging in age from college students to a gray-haired couple, he a retired faculty member, she, his wife'

I started out by asking them to be aware of their presence, to feel their feet touching the floor, to feel the weight of their bodies on their chairs, and so on. Next, I told them that this sense of presence was to be maintained throughout their meditation.

"Sit erect, but comfortably. Watch your breathing. Count your breaths—inhalations and exhalations—one, two, three and four. Then start again at one. Observe that your mind wanders off. Gently return to your breathing and let the other thoughts go."

I picked up the two brass cymbals and clanged them together. The sound reverberated and hung in the air, gradually diminishing.

The twelve of us began our journey inward, each doing as best as he or she could.

We meditated, mostly in silence, but every few moments I reminded these newcomers to "Gently, let your thoughts pass on. Don't follow them. Just be aware that you are the one who is observing these thoughts."

My own thoughts were of Victor. "Where is he? When will he get here? The meditation is almost over. What will I do if he doesn't arrive on time?"

Twenty minutes passed. I called everyone back from wherever they had been by again clanging the cymbals. As the brazen sound-waves diminished I looked around, for our missing teacher. Nowhere. *That means I'm tonight's teacher.* I tried to recall one of Victor's lessons.

"Tonight, I'll speak to you about some of the divisions within each of us. You already heard that we have three centers: the moving center, the emotional center, and the intellectual center. My day job is teaching elementary school and from Victor I've learned that the best classroom lessons I can prepare will appeal to all three of these centers. My goal is to reach the physical moving center, the emotional center, and the intellectual center—ideally, all at the same time."

"But this is only part of the story of how divided you are. You are composed of three centers, any one of which may take over at any given time."

"So who are you? Do you think you know who you are?When you think of yourself as "me" whom are you referring to? Is it one person, or are there several "me"s vying for control of your body? Haven't you ever had the experience of spying a tempting piece of candy sitting on the counter and you say to yourself "No, there are lots of good reasons why I shouldn't eat it" and then as soon as you finish the thought you find your arm reaching out, and in no time the candy is consumed. What just happened? Your body was "me"s. Then, in no time at all, a second me took control. And where were you this whole time? Better yet,I should ask, "Who were you this whole time?"

"You'll find the answer," I continued, "by paying attention; by being aware of what is happening within. The goal of *The Quest* is to show you how to achieve unity, wholeness, to have you function as one complete human being, rather than as the divided person you are now."

By now, as if was on a roll, Victor's ideas just came pouring out of me.

"You all have been here when Victor has called out 'Freeze!' Remember how it was? Do you know what he is teaching you? He's teaching absolute, instant obedience. But why? Not so that he can take over your mind. Just the opposite. It's so that you can develop the strength to take over yourself. The real you should be able to assert itself and resist any of the other 'yous' that are trying to way-lay you from your path."

I'd said everything I'd remembered and still there was no sign of Victor, so I thanked everyone for attending and called the session finished. I went out to my car with a smile on my face, with a sense of relief and of accomplishment.

At home I found Louella in the kitchen and proudly began to tell her about the session.

"Mark, you're a fool," she said. "That man is using you. You're not any 'enlightened being' to tell other people the meaning of life. You may be good at parroting Victor's words, but you don't have any idea of what they mean, do you?"

"Thanks, Louella, you sure know how to deflate a fellow. I was feeling pretty good about what I did tonight and I thought you'd be proud of me."

"I'm sorry," She said. "But you don't expect me to tell you you're right when I know you're wrong, do you?"

"Christ!" I said. "Are you pretending you're my mother. Nothing that I do is good enough. Is it?"

Instead of answering, Louella turned her attention to the pots that lay on the drying board, picked up a towel and began drying one. I turned my back on her and unhappily retreated to the bedroom.

CHAPTER ELEVEN

OVER THE next year I was given more responsibility in The Quest. Victor assigned me my own group of beginners. "Teach them the fundamentals." he said. "How to meditate. Tell them how to become aware of themselves. Then, when you think they are ready, you can send them into one of my more advanced groups."

I felt much less apprehensive facing a group of adults who have freely chosen to attend The Quest than I did, going in every day, to face my own classes at the Lab School. It wasn't that my teaching was going badly. It was a case of never knowing what I was to do next. I approached each day as a six hour stretch of unrelieved anxiety. Arithmetic? It would have been easy to teach straight out of the workbooks, but I knew what a cop-out that would be. The alternative? My own grasp of numbers was sufficiently tentative that I could never convey any of the beauty, or excitement of numbers to my students. In fact, when it came to math, I never felt sure of what I was trying to teach. I knew I was missing the point.

Spelling? I was a serious reader, but I had a limited sense of correct spelling. On one occasion I wrote a word on the board and one of the children said, "Mr. Green, it isn't spelled that way." I looked again. "It seems right to me.... let's vote on it. How many of you think that's the right way to spell the word?"

Even as I was asking for the vote, I knew how outrageous my suggestion was—outrageous, but that's what made it fun!

I don't think I was a bad teacher. Maybe I was even a good one. But I was constantly analyzing the act of teaching. *What does it mean to teach something? I can present a lesson, but that doesn't mean that my children have learned what I just presented. If I teach something to the whole class, some of them will be bored because they already know what I am telling them. A few may be interested, and others will be totally mystified.* I was beginning to suspect that my main function, as a teacher, was to be custodian, a baby sitter, while the children's parents were out doing whatever they had to do. *These kids will grow up, irrespective of what we do in class, and they will learn at their own pace as part of growing up.*

Perhaps Louella could have helped me with the arithmetic, but her kind of math was so far removed from what we were doing in class that I never invited her.

As for her own teaching, she told me, "The math department seems to love me, Mark, and I'm having a ball! Sweetie, this is what I was meant to do! I want to go back and study; first to get my Master's, and probably go on for the Doctorate."

This conversation took place in the afternoon as we walked home from the other side of the campus, where I had met Louella outside the math building.

"Where is it, this school that you want to got to?"

"I've been looking around to see what's out there. The State University, in Columbus has a program that I could start in September. I'd take a room somewhere. Three nights a week, and in just one year I'll be a real math teacher, with a Master's degree!"

"But, do you know what a year in grad school will cost us? We already spend almost as much as we earn. You can't expect to pay tuition out of just my salary can you?"

"That's the wonderful thing." she answered. "My father always told me and my sister that our education is his responsibility. She's married and has kids. She never did go to college, so I'm sure he'll pay for the whole thing."

By now we had reached the main campus crossing. I noticed three attractive young women strolling towards us and immediately my fantasies ran wild. I thought of the possibilities this would open up. "Three nights a week without my wife. Three nights in which to carry on with a limitless number of accessible and beautiful girls, or perhaps with members of The Quest. Who knows what might happen?"

"If that's what you want to do," I said, "then you should do it. You'll become a real mathematician!"

I held Louella's hand and we continued our walk in silence. I thought "This is what they call "mixed emotions." I'm used to having Louella here for me all of the time, and I do like being married to her. And yet...?

September arrived, and Louella's program began. It took me until the second week of her commuting to understand the gulf separating my fantasy life from reality. The reality was that I missed having my wife home with me. The reality also was that the opportunities for illicit, covert liaisons, were not as plentiful as I had imagined. Or perhaps I just didn't know how to go about making them happen?

Louella, however, was having a wonderful time. Each Thursday she came home bubbling over with stories about her professors, her work and her fellow students.

Then, on her third weekend home, I told her "Victor is holding a weekend workshop, starting this Friday evening. We're going off to a Catholic retreat center in Jamestown. Would you like to try it?"

"No. You know I'm not interested in that stuff. And no way could I take off for a weekend. I've got much too much studying. But you go. You'll like it. Go."

That was the answer I'd expected. The invitation was out of politeness, more than with any expectation of bringing Louella back into The Quest.

The retreat was held in a castle-like structure, a monastery perched atop a bluff sloping down to the Ohio River. It was built seventy-five years earlier by the Jesuits for the training of priests. But in these, less orthodox times there was insufficient demand for new priests and the property mostly hosted retreat groups; usually Catholic, but they accepted any group that had a spiritual component: alcoholics anonymous, drug rehabilitation groups, even The Quest.

Fully half of our people showed up for the weekend. We were

each assigned one of the former cells, comfortable but small. Washrooms were at the end of the hall.

Our first evening was spent in meditation, followed by one of Victor's lessons. On Saturday I realized this weekend was going to be dedicated to the physical side of our being, what Victor called "your active center."

Right after breakfast, while the grass was still covered with dew, we stood in a circle, held hands, and swung our arms forward and backwards in time to a chant of nonsense syllables. We did this for maybe fifteen minutes, which felt like an hour. I was thinking "This must look ridiculous to the holy fathers who are walking around the property." Next came an exercise in which we passed a volley-ball from person to person, calling out the name of the intended receiver. By the time we were well exercised, nearly to the point of exhaustion, Victor had us again hold hands, this time in a line. He instructed us to "Hold on." and he led us at a rapid trot through the grounds of the seminary; down the bank-side, along the footpaths covered in fallen leaves, along a riverfront path and then back up the hill to our starting point.

We were puffing hard, and astounded that we each had sum-monsed the energy to complete the run.

Later, at lunch in the cellar dining room, Victor instructed us, "This meal will be consumed in silence please. Each of you will select a tray of food for your neighbor. You are to be 'of service' to that person. Try to remember that, ultimately, service to others is what your life is all about. Now, go—with no talking!"

I was seated next to Rita Robbins, who was one of Victor's long time students. She had two children; a son in the town's public ele-mentary school and a daughter in middle school, yet she still looked like a high school student herself. She was petite, and vibrant. I imagined that, were she still a high school student, surely she would be a football cheerleader.

Silently, I indicated that she should give me her tray. Rita responded with a series of gestures as in a game of charades. The fingers of her left hand galloped across the Formica table top like a prancing animal. Next she pointed the fingers of her right hand, extended, like a gun and aimed at the prancing figure, which then collapsed, turned, so that all five fingers pointed upwards and wiggled weakly. Next, she gestured as though slitting her throat. Her face took on a pained look, her tongue sticking out the corner of her mouth. Finally she extended her two palms towards me in a gesture of rejection. I got it and nodded to her that I understood. I went to the front of the room where cold cuts, salad, breads and drinks were laid out. I, loaded her tray with salads, deviled eggs and celery sticks, bypassing the meat products. I delivered it to her seat and then she went up with my tray, returning with a meal which included the sliced ham and turkey that she had rejected. We ate in silence.

In the afternoon Victor sent me down to the boat dock, telling me to prepare a campfire for our evening's activity. I enjoyed being on my own in the woods, gathering firewood and laying out a ring of stones to confine our fire.

After supper, with flashlights, blankets and a sack of marshmallows, we all went down to the waterfront. The sun was setting as we chose spots around the circle, some spreading blankets on the ground, others perched on rocks or on decaying logs.

I felt myself back in camp. The campfire I built consisted of a tepee of dry sticks placed atop a single sheet of crumpled newspaper. Surrounding the tepee was a log cabin of larger branches. One match and the newspaper flared up, the flames engulfing the tepee.

From time to time I added sticks. The warmth of the fire was already driving off the chilliness, just as our group arrived, descending the forested path and emerging out of the quickly falling darkness.

We encircled the fire-pit, seated on rocks, on logs, or on blankets as Victor spoke about George Gurdjief, his own guru, long deceased, who painstakingly learned the esoteric teachings of the East and brought them to the West. Victor led us in chanting, and we sang a few songs while we toasted marshmallows. Gradually, people began making their way back up the hill, some with flashlights, others relying just on starlight. I added branches to the fire and returned to a spot which was closer to the warmth. I found myself sitting next to Rita Robbins. She had a blue, hand knit poncho around her shoulders but still seemed to be shivering. I found my blanket, nearby on the ground, and wrapped it around both of us. We shared our body warmth. We talked, first about the weekend and then about what had brought us each to The Quest.

"Tell me, Rita," I asked, "isn't your husband at all interested in what we do? Why doesn't he come to any of our events?"

She didn't speak for a moment. She took a deep breath and said, "Mark, you have to understand, my husband is a clarinet player. He plays gigs and he smokes dope. That's all he does. What about your wife, Louella? Why has she stopped coming?"

"I think it's because she has her own interests now. She's so wrapped up in her mathematics."

We talked on and on, then, looking around, I realized we were the only two left sitting by the fire. I added a few more branches. Then I wrapped us more tightly in the blanket. We kissed.

"She's older than I am!" I thought. "She's so much smaller than Louella. Two years I've been married and this is the first time I've held another woman in my arms."

After twenty minutes we got up, stomped out the remaining embers, and hand in hand we went up to the monastery. A couple of times, on our way up the hill, we paused to embrace and kiss.

In the deserted and darkened hall I held Rita, kissed her again, and asked "May I come up to your room with you?"

"No! Certainly not here."

I returned to my room, confused and conflicted. I was pleased with what Rita and I had done. "How exciting! Is this the beginning of a real affair? A new relationship?" Any disappointment I felt at not being invited upstairs and into Rita's bed was offset by my relief at knowing that when I'd get home I wouldn't have too much to conceal from Louella. "It will certainly be easier to face her this way than it would have been if Rita had invited me into her room."

Sunday afternoon I returned home, nervous about what parts of the weekend I could relate to Louella without having my face involuntarily twitch into a nervous grin, revealing what I needed to conceal.

My anxiety, like most anxiety, was unnecessary.

As I entered the front door, Louella looked up from the upholstered chair, put the thick novel she had been reading onto the side table and stood up, grasping the jacket that had also been on her lap. She was dressed in a skirt and sweater, apparently ready to go out somewhere. I tried to embrace her but she rejected my proffered kiss and said, "Finally. At last. I've been waiting and waiting. Otto Mays is in the hospital. He had a heart attack. Hannah is there now and I promised her we would both come, just as soon as you got back."

"What happened? When?"

"Friday afternoon. The same time that you were going off for the weekend. He was lecturing his advanced seminar. He just keeled over. The ambulance took him right to the hospital. I've been there twice, with Hanna. Otto's been in intensive care the whole time."

"Let's go. I'm ready."

We went, immediately, but Professor Otto Mays was dead before we arrived.

CHAPTER TWELVE

WE DROVE Hannah back to her home and Louella took on the hard job of comforting her and attending to her needs. I telephoned the funeral home and began making arrangements.

Two days later Copeland's Funeral Parlor was filled. The oaken sliding pocket-doors had been pushed aside making one large room out of two adjoining rooms, and still people were standing in the back and along the sides. I was pleased to see so many who knew Hannah from The Quest—Al, Rita, and several others, even Victor, despite Hannah's rejection of his behavior. President Hillestad spoke, as did several faculty members. Students spoke about what an inspired teacher Otto had been, but they had even more to say about class picnics that he held on the farm. The rabbi spoke of Otto's heroism in surviving Hitlerism and rebuilding a new and productive life in America.

I didn't speak. Louella and I sat on either side of Hannah, Louella holding her hand through the service.

At the gravesite Victor took me by the arm. "Tell Hannah to come back to us, to rejoin The Quest. It will be good for her. It's what she needs. Otherwise, she is going to be lost."

"Maybe," I said. But I felt put upon. It didn't seem appropriate to raise the question now. "Better you tell her, Victor. You'll have to convince her, if you can."

Victor got no opportunity to speak with Hannah at the gravesite.

Otto's body was interred and then, with each of us taking her by an elbow, we brought Hannah to my car. As we passed through the wrought-iron gates of the cemetery, it occurred to me that my big, black Buick was an appropriate vehicle for this occasion; solemn and dignified. I loved that 1949 car.

We reached the turn off for the Mays' farm. Driving along the quarter-mile lane I was awake to the beauty of the place. The old sugar maples lining the lane were at the peak of their Autumnal display. We passed the chicken coop where the hens, let loose for the day, scratched among fallen leaves and faded grass.

The pasture on one side was fenced to hold the small herd of Black Angus cattle which had been Otto's obsession for the past year.

What is going to happen now? I wondered. How will Hannah manage the farm without Otto....?

Most of us who had been at graveside now gathered at the farm, not only to comfort Otto's widow, but equally to consume well prepared foods and to be happy in each other's company. In my limited experience it seemed that funerals are often more enjoyable than weddings. At weddings there is such pressure to be jolly and to predict nothing but the best for the newlyweds, while at funerals there is no pretense, old grievances are forgotten and there is camaraderie among those who remain and are thankful to be alive.

Several cars were already parked on the grass in front of the farmhouse and when we entered we found food and drinks already set out on the large oaken table. A group of faculty members were already arguing intensely about campus politics. The topic was giving scholarships to "at risk students." That term was a catchphrase for minorities, or blacks. I was interested, so I left Hannah in Louella's company and joined them.

Much later I noticed Victor and Hannah off in an alcove, engaged in what appeared to be serious discussion.

We spent as much time as we could with Hannah for the next few days. Other community members took turns, ensuring that she was rarely alone. One of the tasks I took on was to telephone Otto's cattle dealer and arrange to put the herd of Black Angus cattle at auction. Then, conferring with Hannah, I assured myself that she could handle the rest of the farm chores by herself.

*

The funeral had been on a Tuesday. Eight days later, arriving for Victor's Wednesday class, I was startled to see Hannah there sitting next to Al Kramer, just as in the past, before she had quit, incensed at Victor's infidelity.

How could that be?

Rita Robbins sat in the front row. I considered taking the empty chair next to her but hesitated.

Not in front of Hannah and Al. They'll wonder that I preferred her company to theirs.

So I joined the two of them. We were a trio again: buddies, as we had been a year earlier, before Otto had insisted that his wife have nothing more to do with The Quest.

But why? What brought Hannah back so suddenly? How come she didn't tell me, or Louella, that she was coming back?

There wasn't time to ask. As I was kissing Hannah on the cheek and sitting with my two friends, Victor emerged from a back room, took his accustomed seat facing us, and signaled for silence.

We meditated for only five minutes, then Victor spoke.

"Tonight I will tell you something about which we have not yet spoken. You've begun making a conscious effort to wake up, to be aware of the life you are living. Now I want you to keep an additional thought in your mind. You are to be constantly aware that surely you are going to die."

Victor had much to tell us on this topic. He read us passages from the sages about the importance of holding on to the knowledge that we all were going to die.But it was hard for me to stay focused on his words. I puzzled over Hannah's presence, and I fantasized about Rita, sitting diagonally in front of me. I barely heard a word of Victor's talk.

After class, Hannah, Al and I went together to a coffee shop on Main Street.

"It's really good to have you back with us." Al told Hannah. "I think you did right."

"Well," she answered, "I need to get on with my life. Victor isn't a perfectly realized person. He isn't someone to emulate.... but he's what we have. Otto forbade me to remain in *The Quest*. You both remember that. But Otto is gone, yes? At least, I still have the two of you. You know you're the closest thing to family that's left for me."

"We do love you, Hannah." Al said, taking her hand in his. "You're an inspiration, you know."

I reached out, nodded in approval, and took each of them by their free hand. We three held hands for a long moment, gripping one another tightly, and then, unaccustomed to demonstrating this much emotion, we released our hands and sat silently, until Al spoke.

"And, speaking of family," Al said, "I'm going to have both my daughters visit soon. In two weeks. My ex is finally dating a guy and she actually asked me 'if I would be so good at to take the girls for a couple of days.'"

"Wonderful," Hannah said. "Then, when they get here you'll all have to come out to the farm and I'll meet them. We'll have a Sunday picnic Al, you bring the girls. And Mark, you bring Louella."

CHAPTER THIRTEEN

IT WAS a Thursday afternoon and I anxiously awaited Louella's return from her weekly stint in Columbus. The "crisis" was already in its tenth day and it seemed to be worsening daily. We knew about Soviet missiles, based in Cuba and aimed at The United States. We knew that even more rockets were aboard ships coming this way. We knew that Kennedy and Khruschev were eyeball to eyeball in a game of chicken. But Louella had been so busy studying that we hadn't had more than a couple of brief telephone calls since she went off, Monday morning.

Hearing the Volkswagen pull into the driveway, I hurried out to greet her, embraced her as she emerged from the car, and with my wife back in my arms, I felt noticeably safer.

"No!" I said. "Leave everything be. Come inside. We'll drink, we'll talk. Then I'll help you empty the car."

I poured two glasses of Chianti and we sat.

"Somehow," I said, "I think we'll be okay. This seems to be a good place to wait out whatever is coming.

"Are you really that selfish?" Louella said. "I'm not worried about us. I'm worried about my parents. New York is target number one if we go to war."

"True, but you know Horace Mann College isn't too far from Wright-Patterson Air Force Base. Maybe we're targets too. Still, you know what? Maybe I am learning something from Victor's teachings after all. What will happen will happen. Meanwhile, we live our lives as well as we can. Victor doesn't seem to think that it's our job to fix the whole world. First we have to fix ourselves."

"Mark, you're full of shit! Do you know that?"

I was stung by Louella's words but I just drank my wine in silence.

Three days later, on Sunday we went to Hannah's farm for the promised picnic. Al brought his preteen daughters. It was wonderful to see how pleased he was to have them and to show them off.

Hannah, who had been widowed for nearly a month was a subdued, but gracious hostess.

We ate outside, warmed by the October sun. However the impending war threat was never far from our thoughts. The radio remained on, loud enough so that we shouldn't miss anything new. So it was there, seated outside at the picnic table, we learned that Khruschev had accepted the deal offered by the Kennedy brothers. He agreed to dismantle all the missiles in Cuba and to ship them back to Russia. We Americans agreed to dismantle the missiles we had installed in Turkey, on the Russian border, and we promised never to invade Cuba.

That spring Louella graduated with honors. We celebrated by spending the weekend in Columbus. We stayed in the Hilton hotel and we dined at *L'oie ivre*, which we'd heard was the finest French restaurant in the city.

Louella wore a trim green suit and the white gloves that she always wore on formal occasions.

"You look lovely tonight. Even without the gloves you'd be lovely," I said as we sat down.

"Yes," Louella answered, "But my mother taught me that a lady never appears in public without her gloves." Then she took them off, preparing to eat her meal.

It was magnificent. The friendly service overcame any intimidation which we felt when first facing the menu; totally in French. The wait staff made us feel that we had been feasting and drinking this way our entire lives.

At the end of the meal I raised my glass to Louella. "A toast to you my love, to my graduate, to Louella Green, MS. Master of

Science! You've done it and I'm very proud of you! So now what? Will they hire you at the college? Not just as a teaching assistant, but as a full fledged faculty member? Does everything change now that you have two more letters after your name?"

"Mark, I've been waiting for the right time to talk to you about this. I need to hear what you think."

Louella put down the wine glass which she had dutifully raised in response to my toast. She picked up her water glass and gulped down a large mouthful. "Mark, there were recruiters on campus, two from IBM You know what IBM is don't you?

"Sure, they make typewriters."

"No, that isn't what it's about. Now they're working on computers; machines that can calculate. It's going to be huge, and here I am, right at the beginning. They want me to work in their headquarters, somewhere up the Hudson Valley in New York. Mark, it's a fantastic opportunity!"

"Uh huh. If you're gonna do this, when is it supposed to happen?"

"It's up to me. They want me as soon as I can come."

"And you expect me to quit my job, just like that, and follow you back to New York? You know that I'm finally beginning to enjoy teaching, to feel good about what I'm dong."

"That's why we're talking about it, Mark."

We didn't finish talking about it for nearly a week, at which time Louella enthusiastically accepted the job with IBM. She left for Westchester County the day after we were able to come to an understanding that in a couple of weeks, when my term was over, I would follow her east and we could spend the summer together, then I would return to Horace Mann College and we'd see what happens next.

That was what we decided. We were a loving couple, now we were to live apart—five hundred miles apart.

CHAPTER FOURTEEN

TWO WEEKS after Louella decamped for Westchester County, came my summer vacation and, as planned, I drove east to be with her.

She had leased a second floor studio apartment in Peekskill. The windows looked out across the Hudson River, which was over a mile wide at this spot. The unit was sparsely furnished, mostly through Salvation Army purchases, but the view was superb.

I found Louella bubbling with enthusiasm for her new job.

"Tomorrow," she said, "We'll go to Yorktown Heights and I'll show you what we're doing."

It was a ten minute drive to the IBM facility. She brought me there and led me inside one of the monster computers that, alone, occupied an entire room. Then she showed me what she was currently working on.

"It's called an IBM mainframe "system/360". This machine isn't any bigger than our wardrobe at home, but it's going to replace everything that I've already shown you!"

There was no shortage of things to do while Louella was at work. When good weather called me outdoors I hiked the trails along the river and ascended the peaks of the Hudson Highlands.

The rough green upholstery of the Salvation Army armchair was worn and coffee stained but it was comfortable and I spent hours, hunched there, facing the river, reading novels. I even romped through The Brothers Karamazov which had seemed so tedious when it had been required reading in college.

One weekend we drove out to the tip of Long Island to visit Louella's parents in their country home. We arrived late at night. Joe and Mary Cook had already retired for the night. So, without seeing our hosts, we too went to bed.

We awoke to a fine, sunny morning. Louella's father greeted us. "It's about time you got up. We've been up for hours. I've already been fishing and you are going to enjoy the results, blowfish, just out of the bay! You have to be careful cleaning them though."

"I thought you couldn't eat blowfish."

"If your knife slips and you rupture a bladder you'll be eating poison. But I'm careful. You'll see."

With faith in Louella's father, I thoroughly enjoyed his marvelous coupling of fish, perfectly scrambled eggs and fresh bagels.

Instead of joining the three of us at the breakfast table, Louella's mother, Mary, stood at the sink, sipping coffee. She made sure that we had plenty of juice. She cleared whatever plate or utensil was no longer in use and gave me the uncomfortable feeling that we were constantly under observation.

As soon as the table was cleared Joe took Louella's hand in his two hands and said "Sweetheart, let's you and I walk down to the beach together. There's something I want us to talk about."

They left me alone with Mary. I tried to help her wash the dishes but she shooed me outside. "Go look at the garden." she suggested. "Joe's so proud of his vegetables! Maybe he should have been a farmer and never got himself involved with The Board of Education."

"I'll walk to town and get a newspaper." I said.

"No, don't do that. It's too far."

"Not at all. It's only a mile and a half. I'll enjoy the walk."

"No, It's hilly and it's buggy this time of year. Don't go."

I couldn't understand why Mary Cook was trying so hard to dissuade me, but I went anyway, pausing on my way to appreciate Joe's lush melons, abundant tomatoes, and rows of salad greens.

As I returned, with the unopened newspaper in my hand, Louella met me below the front steps, plainly, upset. *Had she been crying?*

"You haven't read that paper, have you?"

"No." I answered.

"We're going home. Now! Your things are all in the car. Get in the car. Please."

"I'll go up and say goodby and then you'll tell me what's happening."

"No!

Right now. Get in the car!"

We drove off. Louella wasn't crying. She was furious and barely in control of herself.

"Stop the car." she muttered. "Pull over. Right there, onto that lot. Good. Now, here, read for yourself."

I saw the article right away, on the front page, bottom half. Louella's father, Joseph Cook, just yesterday, was indicted, and charged with embezzlement and corruption. The headline read "Board of Education Purchasing Chief arrested." For years, it said, he had been receiving kickbacks before letting contracts for school supplies. Apparently Mr. Cook had been released on bail and was expected to report for trial in the coming week.

"My God! I'm so sorry Louella, for you and for your parents. But what happened just now? Why are we running off this way?"

"Mark, he tried to justify what he did. 'No big deal,' he said. Then he said that he did it for me. For all of us."

"I told him, "Don't you dare put your guilt onto our shoulders, and he said, 'You were happy to have me pay for your education; for college and then for graduate school. How can you claim that you're not a part of it? Then there's your sister, constantly after me for money..."

Louella was silent for a moment. Then she added "He said one more thing in his defense. He said, 'They're all doing it. Everyone at The Board of Ed. Headquarters is on the take.'"

Before I had time to offer any wisdom or consoling thoughts Louella opened the car door, leaned out over the grassy margin and vomited. She was careful and deliberate, managing to soil neither the car nor herself.

I wiped her face with tissues and when she felt herself finished

I restarted the car, steered us back onto the road and we drove on. Louella was crying. I put one arm around her shoulder, drew her towards me and drove much of the return trip steering with one hand.

We were back in our apartment by early afternoon. Louella stood stiffly by the window, looking out across the wide river and at the hills beyond, grimacing, her breath coming in gulps. I stood behind her and wrapped my arms around her. Gradually her breathing approached a normal rate. We stood that way for a long time. Soon she felt the pressure of my erection and responded by pushing against me with gentle circular motions. My hands began to explore beneath her clothes. Then we were together on the wooden floor; clothes somehow discarded. There was an intensity to our lovemaking that was rare for us.

In the weeks that followed I was resolved not to speak about her father unless she spoke first. She never did, but we both followed the course of his trial in the newspapers and on television.

Just before my return to Ohio, to go back to The Lab School, we drove down to New York City for a farewell supper with my parents. They were interested in Louella's work. They wanted to know how I felt about returning to Ohio. We didn't talk about the trial and the subsequent jailing of Louella's father until after supper, when we moved into the living room to drink coffee.

Louella was still hesitant to speak about her father, but my mother insisted.

"I can imagine how hard it is for you. It's a terrible burden, "she said. "But you have to talk about it, dear. You need to sort out all the conflicting emotions you must feel."

"Not at all." Louella answered. "I've made up my mind. The scandal is all his, my father's. It has nothing whatsoever to do with me."

My father, who was busy lighting his pipe, paused, leaned towards Louella, and said, "Really...?"

Louella turned to her father-in-law, fury on her face. She took a deep breath and her features softened. "Why can't I choose to sign off from this? It's none of my doing. God, it's all so simple when I deal with mathematics. Either it's right and it works, or it's wrong and it doesn't work. That's the way the world is supposed to be set up. Isn't it? How come none of you will allow me to live in that kind of a world?"

My father puffed on his pipe, assuring himself that the tobacco had properly caught, then said, "Good question! As you know, Mark's mother and I earn our livings by writing. We have the privilege of taking up moral issues and framing them however we choose. We can even bypass them when it suits our purpose. But to tell you the truth, the kind of mathematically perfect world that you want to live in doesn't seem to work, even in fiction. This is a tough one that you're facing. I wish you all the strength you can find to work your way through it."

Parting from my parents that night my mother said, "Mark, drive safely, have a wonderful year in Ohio, and good luck to both of you in working out this crazy separation. I hope you both know what you're doing. And Louella, for God's sake, don't be shy. You know we want you to visit us whenever you can make it to the city."

Two days later, early afternoon, I found myself half way home, well into the Pennsylvania Turnpike. I became aware of a palpable shifting of perspective. Louella, her father's troubles, her work, that incomparable view from the stained easy chair—all the things I'd been thinking about—I felt them slip away as the details of the life awaiting me in Cold Springs, at Horace Mann College, crept into my thoughts and possessed me.

Only then did it occur to me, after two months, how far I had gotten from Victor's teachings; that in the whole summer I hadn't once stopped to consciously recollect my presence—certainly not to sit down to meditate. Still, it was with pleasure that I looked forward to rejoining The Quest. My thoughts about the new school year were more complicated: *It will be good to see the kids again, only half of my class has moved on to the middle school and I already know the incoming kids, so that's no problem. But each day is still going to feel like a personal challenge. What will I do to fill up the time. How will they receive whatever I have to offer? On the one hand, I know that I am up to the challenge.... and yet?*

I wasn't nervous about returning to an empty house. The experience of Louella's going off to Graduate School for three nights a week hadn't been so bad. *We'll see how this goes.*

Crossing the state line, leaving Pennsylvania and entering West Virginia, I found myself rehearsing Victor's teachings. *Enough idle speculation. Here and now. Pay attention to this moment. Wake up! Be aware of where you are, who you are and what you are doing right now.*

I kept it up for maybe fifteen minutes but then I tired of the effort. I turned the radio on to station WWVA, Wheeling, West Virginia and immersed myself in bluegrass. As evening came on the brilliant red and orange hues of the sunset were lovely. I then remembered Victor Lamotta telling us not to listen to the car radio. Rather we should keep our attention on 'the working surface' which, in this case, was the automobile tires meeting the road. Nonetheless, country and western music brought me most of the way home.

CHAPTER FIFTEEN

DESPITE LAST night's late arrival I awoke at six in the morning, flung my arm to the side, reaching for my wife, and was surprised to find myself alone, but in my own—sometimes *our* own—familiar bed.

A couple of coffee refills helped pass the time until it felt late enough to check in with Hannah. Then, when I called to let her know I was back,

it wasn't Hannah who answered the phone. Instead, Victor Lamotta's familiar voice said, "Hello, this is the Mays' farm. May I be of service?"

"Victor! It's Mark Green, back from New York. Hello. But I wasn't expecting to reach you at Hannah's. How are you? Was it a good summer? What's happening?"

"Do you really want me to answer your questions or do you want to talk to Hannah?"

"Well, both, I guess. I just got back last night. You tell me how you and Gertrude are and then I'll talk to Hannah."

"No, you can't talk to Hannah right now because she's away for the weekend. Why don't you come here, out to the farm. We'll have some coffee together and I'll bring you up to date."

"I'll be there in half an hour, Victor."

I went directly to the farm but before driving up to the main house I paused at the barn to visit with my goat Ruthie who, again, had been a summer boarder. I found her lying down in the pen where Hannah kept her goats and sheep. Ruthie came right up to me and offered to let me scratch behind her ears.

"Good to see you, old girl! Hannah took good care of you, didn't she? Are you ready to come back to school with me? How's about I come and get you in a couple of days?"

Not expecting any answer from Ruthie, I got back into my car and moved on to park next to the farmhouse.

I found Victor, on Hanah's porch, seated in one of the four Adirondack chairs. Victor didn't immediately give me any recognition. He continued to read in his book until he came to the end of a paragraph. Then he looked up."Welcome home!" he said, rising slowly and wrapping me in a hug, a surprisingly warm hug coming from such a slender man.

"Victor, you're the one who looks 'at home' here. What's happening?"

"Come inside. Coffee's hot and I'll tell you everything."

Coming into Hannah's large farmhouse kitchen I saw that the wooden plank table was set for twelve places. Hannah had never been much of a housekeeper, but now the room was tidy and spotless. There were vases with wildflowers on the table as well as on the counters, and in one corner of the room a shelf had been made into some sort of shrine. It held a small, golden statue of the Buddha and in front of the Buddha was a lit candle.

Victor, in his customary deliberate manner, poured our coffee. I knew his injunction to "do only one thing at a time, and do it with full attention and awareness," so I too said nothing until the coffee was poured and I had added cream and sugar. Victor drank his coffee black.

We brought our mugs out onto the porch and when we were seated, out of politeness, I first asked about Gertrude.

"She's working, early as it is, she's out giving a massage," Victor said. "You know Gertrude has graduated and is a licensed therapeutic masseuse now. But you are here to ask me about Hannah, to find out why she's back with us, and for that matter, why we are here on the farm."

"Darn right! Where is she, anyway?"

"Hannah is fine. She went off to Chicago for a couple of days; shopping, theater, the works! So let me tell you exactly what happened."

"No, first tell me. Did she go by herself?"

"Stop imagining things, Mark. I sent someone with her, to keep an eye on her. She's fine. They're coming back tonight—or maybe tomorrow."

"Good. Now fill me in. What's happening?"

"It was a momentous summer, for all of us. I believe that The Quest, and my personal sessions with Hannah, are the only thing that's been holding her together since her husband, the professor, died. She and I talked a lot. Her biggest worry was how she could manage the farm all by herself. But she couldn't imagine living anywhere else either. We talked a lot. One day, while I was visiting her, here at the farm, Hannah suggested, all by herself, that maybe this was the best place for me—for The Quest—in which to do our work. One of the things she said: 'Think of the times you've had us on our hands and knees polishing the floor at the church annex. The way things are now, we'll polish those floorboards till they shine like mirrors and they'll still belong to the church. And why should you all go away to a retreat center when you could come here instead? Look at all the unused buildings and space that we have right here!'"

"Do you mean your'e renting the place? With Hannah still living here?"

"So much has happened while you were away," Victor continued. "Gertrude and I are living upstairs, in one of the bedrooms. You see the camper?" Victor pointed to a small mobile home, set up on cement blocks, which had escaped my notice. "Your friend Al Kramer brought it here. He's away this week, but he'll move in when he gets back for the new semester. All together, there are seven of us living on the farm. But others come for meals at certain times. You probably saw that the kitchen table is set for twelve. You are welcome to come and join us for supper tonight if you wish."

I sighed, looked around, put my now empty coffee cup down on the arm of my wooden chair, and tried to assimilate Victor's words.

"It's a big step forward for The Quest." Victor continued. "We can achieve so much more, here in this space. You'll be amazed. And you, Mark, you are going to be a big part of it."

I felt the intensity of Victor's full attention as he said, "This is what you need, Mark."

I wasn't ready to respond to his last remark. Instead, as I stood up, I told Victor that I couldn't come that evening. "Too much to do. But may I show up tomorrow?" I asked.

"Surely."

I started to go to my car when Victor stopped me.

"Mark, you're not going to leave your coffee cup sitting there for somebody else to clean, are you?"

I spent the afternoon and evening preparing lesson plans for my classes about to start. Then I telephoned Louella in Peekskill.

After hearing my report Louella said, "What do you mean, Mark, you're telling me you asked how much he is paying Hannah and he wouldn't tell you?"

"No. I didn't say 'he wouldn't tell me.' Just that he didn't tell me."

"Mark, be careful. He's a manipulator. You have to protect Hannah."

"She's a grown woman, Louella. She's seen much more of the world than we have. I suspect she knows what's best for herself."

"You do, huh? I don't know. Keep your eyes wide open Mark, please."

Then Louella told me a bit about her next assignment; something about a new language: a new way to talk to the computer. I tried to understand what it was about but her explanation was beyond me. All that I grasped was that she enjoyed her work and she liked her co-workers.

When I hung up from talking with my wife I had a powerful desire to call Rita Robins and to see if we could rekindle our flirtation. I sat in the silent living room, looking at the telephone. What if her husband answers? What will I say to him? Maybe one of her children will answer? Maybe she doesn't want to talk to me? I mentally rehearsed her telephone number. Once I even picked up the receiver. But I didn't dial the number.

CHAPTER SIXTEEN

THE SUN was low in the sky when I arrived for supper at the farm. Hannah must have seen my car drive in because as I climbed the porch stairs the front door opened and she came out to greet me. We embraced. She seemed grayer, frailer than I remembered her.

"It's so good to see you!" I said. "But so much has happened in the time I was gone, Hannah. You need to tell me everything."

Before she could answer, Gertrude and Victor also came through the door to welcome me. Gertrude kissed me on the cheek and asked after Louella. I noticed that Gertrude's weight hadn't gone down any since I last saw her. Victor followed my gaze and said, "She's beautiful, isn't she!"

We all went indoors. I recognized the skinny, dark haired girl who had once sanded floors with me. She sat at the table next to a three-year-old boy. "Hello, Mark. This is my son, Zachary," she said. I couldn't remember her name but later recalled that it was Laura Steiner, and yes, I clearly remembered my enthrallment as I peeked at her vigorously swaying breasts.

Hannah gestured that I should take the empty place next to Laura. Hannah sat at one end of the table, Victor and Gertrude sat at the other end. One more couple sat across from Laura and me; Jeremy and Patricia O'Hara, long time pupils of Victor's whom I hardly knew. They were a few years older than I, in their early thirties. Jeremy was a pudgy real estate lawyer who commuted into Springfield every day. Patricia, much more vibrant than her husband, taught kindergarten in the public school.

These six, plus Al (who was away) were the current residents of the farmhouse. I was the only guest that evening.

Before we ate we held hands around the table and Victor said,

"We are grateful to be here together and we welcome Mark back into our midst. We offer blessings and thanks to the life that died so that we might eat, flourish, and grow. Amen."

Gertrude and Patricia went to the open kitchen counter and returned to the table with platters of food.

"You know, you picked a good night to rejoin us." Victor told me. "After supper we're having a workshop on 'the movements.' Jeremy spent all of July in Texas learning them. That's quite an achievement and tonight he's showing us what he's learned."

Jeremy was obviously pleased at Victor's approval. "You know, Mark," he intoned, "when people asked Gurdjief what his trade was, he would describe himself as 'a dealer in Persian carpets and a dance teacher.' He learned the dances himself when he was a young man. He traveled into the lands of the whirling dervishes, sure that somewhere, in some remote location known only to the initiated, there existed a school which taught traditional wisdom, the truths that he sought. Gurdjief found the esoteric schools that he was looking for, learned what they had to teach him, and brought the teachings back to the West."

Jeremy was warming to his topic, going on to tell how proud he was to have a part to play in transmitting this essential part of Gurdjief's teachings.

"Victor sent me out to Texas, to a commune outside of Dallas, where he knew that the movements are practiced. Victor told me that this is the one part of the teachings that we're missing, here in The Quest."

My mind wandered away from Jeremy's words. I looked around the table and saw Jeremy's wife, Patricia, demonstrating her boredom by toying with her food, picking up a spoonful of peas from her plate and then spilling them one by one onto her mashed potatoes.

On my right, Laura Steiner, her back to me, sliced her son's meat.

When Jeremy came to a pause in his monolog I turned to Hannah and said, "Well, Hannah, Jeremy visited a commune in Texas, but it seems that you are establishing your own commune, right here. Is that what you want your farm to become?"

"Not really," she replied, putting down her fork and giving me her full attention. "No. What Victor is building here isn't a commune. It's a school. People won't be coming here to 'do their own thing.' They'll be coming to learn a better way of living in this world."

Now Victor entered our conversation.

"Hannah is doing a wonderful thing, allowing us to create a living school on her farm. But she's doing a wonderful thing for herself, at the same time."

It was at this moment that I became aware of Laura Steiner's leg pressing against my leg. An accident? Does it mean anything? I had to find out. I put my right hand onto my own knee. In the process my fingers lightly brushed Laura's thigh. Her hand also went below the table, next to mine. She gave my hand a warm squeeze and then resumed feeding her son. To my pleasure, for the rest of the meal, our legs kept returning, pressing, one against the other.

I helped to clear the tables. Patricia and Hannah were in charge of washing the dishes. Laura went off to put her son, Zachary, to bed.

After the supper dishes were finished and I had put two and a half dollars into the wicker basket on the kitchen counter, we all walked over to the barn, climbed the steps into the nearly empty hay mow, which Victor now used as a classroom, a theater, a meeting place, or on this night, as a workshop on the movements.

Victor's students began arriving even as Jeremy and I were setting up benches in a large circle. Nearly thirty people had arrived and we were about to begin when I saw the person whom I had been looking for the whole time, Rita Robbins. She looked lovely. She was wearing the same pale blue poncho that she had on the night of the campfire, our one night of affectionate cuddling at the retreat center; the night that I had obsessed about ever since. I approached her. "Rita, it's been a whole summer. I've missed you."

She responded by giving me a light kiss on the cheek.

"Hello Mark," she said. "Al's here too. He just got back from visiting his daughters. He's parking the car. He'll be so happy to see you!"

As she spoke my friend Al Kramer came up the steps. He approached us, his eyes twinkling, his radiant smile not at all hidden by his bushy beard and long curly hair. He towered over me and greeted me with one of his familiar bear hugs.

Al released me from his grip, put his arm around Rita, and said to me, "You know that Rita left her husband and she's coming to live with me, in the Winnebago."

I hoped that my face betrayed no emotion at the sudden foreclosure of my fantasies. "What about your kids?" I asked Rita.

"For now they are with their father. I didn't want to take them out of their school. We'll see."

Jeremy put on a record, a slow Middle Eastern tune. First we heard chanting. Then there were flutes, drums, tambourines, and unrecognized string instruments.

Jeremy, standing in the center of the circle, performed a series of seemingly unconnected movements of his arms and his legs.

At the end of the record, still standing, Jeremy began his lecture. He repeated much of what he had said earlier at the supper table.

"These movements aren't easy," he said. "You know what they're like? Remember when you tried to rub your belly with one hand and tap the top of your head with the other hand, then somebody would say 'switch' and you'd have to tap your belly and rub the top of your head. Well, that's a simplified example of what you'll be learning here. It takes exquisite attention. There is no way that you can do these movements and let your mind stray onto anything else."

"There's an even simpler task that turns out to be almost as hard." Jeremy said. "Let's all try it. Hold your hands out, chest level. Point your index fingers, one at the other. Circulate your left hand in a clockwise direction. Keep it circulating, and now circulate the other hand in a counter-clockwise direction."

We all tried. There were grimaces. There was laughter. But nobody had much success.

"You'll have to concentrate," Jeremy said. "These movements will take you a long way towards the goal of self observation and self awareness. And if we learn to move in unison, you'll see, we generate an astounding amount of high quality energy. Think of the whirling dervishes who can keep at the dance for hours and hours."

Jeremy was right. It was hard. Never before had I felt so clumsy, so uncoordinated as when I tried to twirl my fingers in opposite directions.

"OK, everyone stand up.... I'll play the record again and you all try to follow me."

We tried, with mixed success.

Then the lesson was over and I went right down the steps and out, without saying 'goodnight' to Al, to Rita, to Victor, to Hannah or to anyone.

I was disappointed that Laura, after putting her son to bed, hadn't bothered to come learn the movements.

CHAPTER SEVENTEEN

SCHOOL OPENED. *My fifth year already! Amazing.* Driving up to the flat-roofed cinderblock building, built in 1953, I felt comforted by the familiar presence. The three classrooms, Louie's office and the common room had also come to feel like home. Louie, the Principal, and nominally my boss, was a full professor in the Horace Mann Education Department.I was still an instructor. Since education students from the college regularly student taught in my classroom, my teaching in the lab school gave me faculty status, even if it didn't put me on the tenure track. Louie's office sat between Helen's combined third and fourth grades and my own fifth and sixth. Two walls of his office were taken up with one-way mirrors, making it possible for Louie to occasionally crowd an education class in there, where, silent and unobserved, they could watch Helen or me teaching.

I returned to the twice-a-week faculty volleyball game to discover that Dr. Lacy, whom I now addressed as 'Tom' still had a wicked serve but it was becoming easier to return. *Either my game has improved or his had slowed down.*

Louella and I spoke on the phone most nights. I called her that Friday to report on my first week of school.

"Do you like this year's kids?" Louella asked.

"They're fine. Half of them are returning from last year, and I already knew the ones that Helen sent up to me, so it hardly feels like a new year. It feels more like taking up right where we left off."

"And what about The Quest?"

"Victor's got me teaching two groups now, two nights a week, beginners and intermediates."

"That's too much, isn't it? You know, you don't owe that man your whole life."

"I like it, Lou. I know, you think it's a cult. But it doesn't seem that to me. So far it all makes sense."

"I can't understand the hold Victor has over all of you. He's got you doing his teaching, he's got Hannah to give over her farm to him, he's got the lot of you to scrub, paint and perform for him...."

Louella was still speaking when I became aware that I had just lost control of myself. I'd intended to apply Victors's teachings throughout our conversation. I wanted to keep myself in mind, from the time that I reached out to dial Louella's number until the end of our call. My intention was to be self-aware throughout our talk. I wanted to visualize myself, first talking, and then listening. I tried to follow Victor's instructions: "Listen with full attention; hear without editing, or considering; don't plan what you are going to say next while someone is speaking to you. Just listen. Wait till it is your turn and then the necessary words will come by themselves."

I felt myself criticized. I lost it. From the time when Louella started to complain about The Quest, our conversation deteriorated into what Victor would describe as "a mechanical state of sleep."

"Enough, Louella. No more about The Quest. I don't want to talk about it any more. You tell me how your project is going. Are you involved in anything besides work?"

Louella spoke at length about her mentor Joe Rizzo, to whom she had once introduced me. She said she and Joe were assigned to the same project and that, essentially, she was his assistant. She spoke about how much he was teaching her, how they sometimes become so involved in the intricacies of their work that they would continue in the lab well past the end of the work day. "Sometimes," she said, "Joe takes me out to supper because it's already too late for him to go home to eat with his wife and kids. Joe has invited me to come to his home tomorrow for lunch. He says that his wife has been wondering about this woman he's spending so much time with and she wants to meet me."

"That should be interesting." I said. "Okay, Louella, We've talked long enough. I do miss you. Even if it's only been a couple of weeks. I do miss you. But now I want to go to bed."

"Okay, love. Hang in there. Remember, they're giving me a whole week off, second week in November, in exchange for my keeping things going here over Thanksgiving. It'll be so nice to spend it back in our own home again."

It was nearly two months before her holiday arrived. I drove to Cincinnati to meet Louella's flight and, as a joke, I held up a card-board sign that read "Mrs. Louella Green." Maybe it wasn't really a joke? Standing at the barrier separating arrivals from those waiting, I scanned the face of each woman ascending the walkway. It became harder and harder to call up exactly what she looked like or to imagine what she might be wearing.

Then I saw her. She had on a green knit skirt and jacket. Her white blouse was buttoned up to the neck. She had on a white pillbox hat and she wore her white gloves.

I thought that she looked lovely.

"You didn't need that silly sign," she said. "I'd of known you anywhere."

We embraced and kissed.

"I'm so glad that you came back to me." I said.

We had wonderful sex that night. We pleasured each other in new ways. We came together again and again; something I hadn't even known I was capable of.

There were moments, during our lovemaking, when I thought, "Has she learned new techniques from Joe Rizzo, or from anyone else in Yorktown Heights?" The thought might well have stifled my passion, but it didn't.

Before falling asleep I told myself, "Wherever she learned her skills, whoever she may have slept with, I have no grounds to complain. After all, I've been sleeping with Laura. In fact, maybe I'm the one who has brought something new to our bed."

I recalled the times Laura and I had met in the hayloft, starting the very next night after she had aroused and teased me, leg-to-leg, at the supper table. I visualized the first time we made love, how hurried it was, Laura afraid to stay too long out of earshot of her sleeping son. The second time, while Zachary was visiting a play-mate, we had more time, but our coupling was still brief and as we left the barn Laura remarked "You know how to satisfy a woman, don't you? But there are still things I need to teach you."

The next time we met in the hayloft her instructions began.

I had one more thought before falling asleep, positioned like spoons with Louella. I was pleased to realize that my wife's tiny and pointed breasts excite me just as much as Laura's full breasts.

All week, while I taught school, Louella was busy reestablishing her cold springs persona.

At breakfast she told me "The one I most want to see is Gertrude." I feel so distant from her, ever since she moved in with Victor. I hope we are still friends. I'm not sure."

On Tuesday Louella's old colleagues in the math department invited her to come and speak to them about her work at IBM.

"They want to know what's going on in 'the real world.'" she said.

Late that afternoon Louella came back from her talk, pleased and excited.

"They're a lovely bunch of people, the Math Department," she said,"but they live in a completely different world from the one I'm living in. They were full of the most naive questions. Professors! Ph.D.s! I'm beginning to think the gulf between academia and cor-porate life is wider than they'll ever know."

"Do you miss academia?" I asked.

"Not much. You know, they kept asking me when I'm going to come back—back to the department, and they even asked me when I was going to come back to my husband."

"What did you tell them?"

"That I'm 28 years old already, so it needs to be sooner, rather than later, if we're going to have children and if my husband will still have me back, then I'll come home. Meanwhile, though, I feel like I'm in the very center of things, right on the cutting edge: it's mathematics as a real-world tool. I can't give it up just now. Anyway, that's how I answered them"

I got up from the kitchen table, put my arms around her, and said, "Of course I want you back, full time, Louella…. I expect that when you get around to coming home I'll still feel that way."

The next day I telephoned, inviting Hannah to dinner.

She insisted we should come out to the farm.

"There's no reason Louella should bother to cook. Why don't you just come here to dinner? There's always plenty of food, good company, and then we'll sit and talk."

"Wait a moment." I handed the receiver to Louella.

"No, Hannah," Louella told her. "Thanks, but in the first place, we want you to be our guest, and in the second place I want to talk to you, not to all those other people."

Hannah came to us, and when she did, I poured martinis for the three of us.

"You remember, Hannah? It was your husband, the renowned Doctor Otto Mays, who taught me how to drink these wonderful things."

"He did love them." Hannah said. "Otto sometimes used to say that he missed pre-war Germany terribly, but that he had to come to America to discover martinis. He felt that martinis went a long way towards making up for the loss of our homeland."

"It's been over a year already, hasn't it?" I asked.

"A year and three weeks, precisely," Hannah answered.

We raised our martini glasses; "To Otto!" I said. "A wonderful man, and a good friend."

Louella and I, but mostly Louella, spent the remainder of dinner trying to pry out of Hannah exactly how she felt about giving over her farm to The Quest. Apparently, despite Louella's fears, Hannah was perfectly content.

"Victor takes care of the property. He makes sure that the grass is cut, that the hay gets mowed, and that the animals are fed. Gertrude pays the bills."

"Who pays the taxes?" I asked.

"I'm still paying the taxes," Hannah answered. "But every month I get a social security check and that's enough to take care of it."

"What about food?" I asked.

"We have a committee that plans the menus and buys the food. Then we each pay our share."

"What about the rent that the other tenants pay?" Louella asked.

"I don't really know about that." Hannah said. "I don't have to pay rent. I assume the money that the others pay goes towards the work of The Quest."

Hannah stayed till nine O'clock, which she insisted was her bedtime.

We both walked her outside, to the driveway where she had parked her yellow Toyota pickup truck. We each kissed her goodbye and I said, "Tomorrow we'll come to you for supper. Thursday is one of the evenings that I meet with my beginners class so we'll come early and eat with you."

Thursday morning I went off to school early, leaving my wife still asleep.

A bit after ten that morning, as I stood in front of my class, presenting a new writing assignment, the door opened and there was Louella. Clearly, she was agitated. Instead of entering she insistently beckoned me to step outside. I went and she whispered, "President Kennedy has just been shot."

"What! When?"

"No. That's all that I know. The radio's on in the car, but they don't have anything to say yet. I'm going to tell the other teachers," and she turned away from me.

I backed into the room, faced the class and had no idea what would be the appropriate thing to say. In truth, I was equally confused about what my own reaction was, or should be. *How not to alarm them? Am I alarmed? Is it my business to tell them? How can I not tell them?*

I walked to the front of classroom, approached the blackboard and picked up a stick of chalk. Before I had time to do anything more, two of the class mothers pushed through the door, come to claim their children and take them home. Mrs. Kendell, the first one in, looked at me questioningly, holding up her hands in a gesture of indecision and then beckoned to her son to come to her.

Looking out at the parking lot I saw more cars approaching.

"All right," I said aloud. "Maybe you all know. President Kennedy is in Dallas, Texas. Apparently, somebody shot him. We don't know anything more than that. Not yet. Some of your parents will want to have you home with them, as the details come in. Meanwhile, we'll turn on our radio and learn what's happening."

We turned on the radio and heard speculation that the President was not likely to survive.

More parents kept driving up to the school to take their children home. By noon the class was empty and the world knew that President Kennedy was dead.

"Louella, let's drive out to Hannah's farm. We can watch television there as easily as in our own home. We'll see how Hannah is doing and we can find out what everyone else is thinking."

As we drove to the farm I was comforted by the knowledge that Laura wouldn't be there. She had already left to take little Zachary to visit her parents, his grandparents, in Texas. I was glad to avoid being in the presence of both my wife and my sometimes-girl-friend. We found Hannah, Gertrude and Patricia mesmerized by the television reports.

"Where's Victor?" I asked.

"He's upstairs in our room, doing some writing." Gertrude answered. "He said we can call him if anything else happens, or if Kennedy comes back to life."

"We're canceling tonight's classes, aren't we?"

"You'll have to ask Victor."

I went up the steps and knocked on the door to Victor and Gertrude's bedroom.

"Come in, if you have anything to tell me," he called out.

"Victor, do you want me to phone around and tell people not to come this evening?"

"No Mark. What I want you to do is to call everyone and tell them, by all means, they should show up tonight. You have to know what is important; what is real, and what is just an idea you hold in your head, based on some notion that somebody once told you."

Victor's words puzzled me, but I made the telephone calls as he had instructed.

When it was time for me to meet with my group Louella remained with Gertrude, watching the news on television.

I was pleased to see all twelve of my beginners appear on time.

"You did right to come." I told them. "It's better than the alternative of watching the story repeat itself incessantly on the tv screen. Now I'll lead you through the exercise of connecting to your body. We'll meditate for twenty minutes or so, and then I want to talk to you about how to relate today's events to your real lives."

In my speech I tried to mimic Victor's words, which I had been thinking about for the past several hours. I talked about how, as we grow up, "personality" comes to replace "essence". We accrue a mass of ideas; and they are all wrong. They have nothing to do with reality.

From there I pretty much winged it, trying to make the connection between self awareness and the ability to avoid being controlled by runaway imagination.

When my talk was over I left the barn and returned to the main house, to pick up Louella and go home. Once we were seated in the Buick, even before we pulled out onto the road, Louella said, "Gertrude is pregnant. She hasn't told Victor yet. She's afraid to. She doesn't know how he'll react. She's pretty sure that his wife will never give him a divorce. His wife is Catholic and she's furious at Victor. What a combination!"

"Does she want the baby?" I asked.

"That's a stupid question, Mark."

"No it isn't. She doesn't have to have the baby. You know that."

"Okay. You're right, it isn't a stupid question. It's an unfeeling question. And anyway, yes, she does want to have Victor's baby."

Two days later, on Sunday, it was time for Louella to fly east. On our way to the airport we stopped at the farm so that she could say one more goodbye.

We parked, left the car and went up the porch steps. I was about to knock when Louella said, "Don't bother knocking. It isn't Hannah's house any more. It's become a public institution."

I turned the doorknob. "I suppose you're right. I'll try to ignore the sarcasm in..."

Before I could complete the thought we found ourselves entering bedlam. The three women living in the farmhouse, Hannah, Gertrude and Patricia, were on the stuffed couch facing the television set, which blared at high volume. Hannah was shouting. Gertrude and Patricia were trying to quiet her.

Seeing us, Hannah screamed "It's the Reichstag. It's the Reichstag all over again. I've been there in Germany and now it's happening here!"

"What's happened?" I asked.

Hannah removed Gertrude's arm, then Patricia's arm, from her shoulders. She pushed herself up from the couch and threw her arms around me.

"There's no place left to run to, Mark. No place to get away from them. They do what they want. They lie. They torture. They kill. They're in charge and they'll get what they want."

Hannah was struggling to get her words voiced in between the sobs that rocked her body.

In my loudest voice, I demanded, "Will anyone please tell me what's happening?"

Patricia answered me. "It's Lee Harvey Oswald. He's been shot dead."

"By the same people who shot Kennedy," Hannah shouted. "First they killed the President. Then they framed poor Oswald.

They said he's a communist and then they killed him. Next they are coming after us, I promise you."

Victor came into the room. He looked at each of us a deliberate, slow, penetrating look, then he took Hannah by the hand and led her into the dining room, where he sat her down and placed himself in a chair facing her. I marveled. I'd never before seen him so gentle.

"Hannah," he said, holding both her hands across the table, "take a couple of deep breaths. That's better. Now breathe regularly. Be here. Be in 'the now'. The universe is a very big place, Hannah. Everything feeds on energy. Every death releases energy back to the universe. We feed from that energy and the way we do it is through attention. Let go of your ideas and just be here. Breathe deeply. Follow your breath. That's better, much better"

Still holding Hannah's hands, Victor turned to Louella, who had followed them into the dining room.

"So you're going back East, Louella, we wish you well there."

"Thank you Victor." Louella said as she removed Victor's hands from Hannah's, bent down and embraced her distraught friend. Hannah managed a smile, stood up and returned the hug. "Don't stay away so long this time. I'll be here for you when you get back," Hannah said.

Having said our goodbyes to everyone we got into my old Buick and headed for the airport.

"Mark, going back to work is going to feel like a vacation after this week."

"Shush," I replied, "I'm listening to the news."

CHAPTER EIGHTEEN

A MONTH later I joined my wife in Peekskill for the Christmas holidays.

I found her as enthusiastic about her job as ever. She seemed pleased to have me with her, though clearly, my presence wouldn't be allowed to interfere with her work.

The third morning, a Saturday, I got up from the breakfast table, poured myself a second cup of coffee, sat down again and said, "Put down your paper, Louella. Listen, please. I want to talk about your father. I think it's time that you relented. You need to go see him. For God's sake, It's Christmas. He's only a few miles away, in Sing Sing. He's got four years left on his sentence. Why not ease his pain a little bit? You'll feel better too, about yourself, I mean."

She turned to me, and with no hesitation, said what she had long been saying, "Mark, you know why I haven't had anything to do with Dad. It's about standards; expectations, the way we're supposed to live in this world." Then she threw her newspaper to the floor and stared out, across the Hudson River. After a thoughtful silence she turned back towards me and continued, "Still, you know what I'm beginning to believe? Those standards are crumbling—everywhere. Damned if I want to be the last one standing, trying to defend some morality that nobody else lives by."

On the afternoon of Christmas Eve Louella put on her business suit and a pair of white gloves and then I drove her to the main gate of Sing Sing, where her mother and sister, each wearing similar white gloves, were waiting for her. I watched them as they disappeared behind the massive stone walls. I stayed, waiting, in the parking lot, looking out across the Hudson at its widest: The Tappan

Zee. I marveled that inmates should be housed in such a spectacular location, though, most likely, I guessed, few of their cells had windows opening onto this panorama of water and mountains.

A week later I flew home, pleased that Louella had begun to shed the anger which she felt towards her father, a burden which she had been carrying for over a year.

I ate most of my dinners and weekend meals at the farm and I continued teaching there two nights a week. On a third night we "old timers" received more advanced instruction from Victor. I sensed that he no longer viewed me as the anointed one. Maybe he saw a tentativeness in my commitment, or perhaps a lack of unquestioning loyalty. Instead of me, it was Jeremy who seemed to have been picked for that role. Jeremy basked in Victor's approval, first as the one who had gone to Texas and brought back the esoteric dances, then as the one who would manage things whenever Victor was away. I was quite content to relinquish my place, as the chosen one—if indeed it ever was my place.

Al and Rita lived together in the Winnebago. Al and I were still close, though I seldom spoke to Rita. I was fairly confident that she hadn't told Al about our brief encounter that night at the campfire. In truth, my infatuation was completely a thing of the past. By now I realized that the whole thing existed basically in my fantasy life.

Now it was with Laura Steiner that I satisfied those fantasies and happily for me, she was willing to meet me in secret, and never to display any public affection.

The farm's population was expanding. Several consecutive work-weekends had converted the old chicken coops into four apartments. It was seldom that all twelve places at the kitchen table weren't fully occupied, and now, two years after his death, Otto Mays' extensive library of physics and mathematical texts was boxed and carried up to the attic. The library became additional dining space.

One afternoon, after the day's teaching, I drove to the farm for supper. Seeing me approach, Victor rose from the porch, and came down the steps to meet me. He took me by the arm and said, "Mark, come walk with me. I have something I want to talk about with you."

We strolled and he said, "I've decided we should have a school here, on the property, an elementary school, for young children. I want you to run it. That's what is best for you, I'm sure. Here you'll be able to teach what is true and real. Your work in the Lab School isn't accomplishing anything significant, but this will."

I bristled at his words. "*There he goes again, demeaning me, making sure I know that everything I do is worth nothing. And I'm not going to object. I can't. There's no questioning Victor's pronouncements from on high*"

I felt myself drawing down into the same safe spot to which I'd retreat to each time I felt Louella belittling me, implying that I'm performing at less than my full capacity.

Not expecting an answer, Victor continued,

"You know Gertrude is going to give birth to my baby any day now. I can already see him growing and learning, right here on the farm; growing into a genuine human being. And you are a big part of that vision, of his growth.

"No, Victor," I said. There was no hesitation in turning down his proposition. I was proud of my willingness to protect myself from his design and to react unequivocally. "I'm not the one to run your school. I love what I do at the Lab School. But you're right. It's a good idea, making The Quest available to young kids, including your own. But why not Patricia? I hear she's a wonderful teacher. She's full of enthusiasm. She'd be just right for the job, wouldn't she?

"I suppose she would."

"And her husband could come in and teach the movements," I added. "Clearly, he hates doing real estate law. He'll be much happier staying here, helping you teach classes and helping his wife run the school."

Our work projects, for the rest of the year, consisted of transforming the hay barn into a school house which, under Patricia's direction, would open in the Fall.

*

With the hay barn no longer available for farm purposes, freshly cut and baled hay was now stacked in the wagon shed. One June evening Laura Steiner and I lay there, atop the stack.

There was a delicious combination of warm, moist air mixed with the fragrance of the hay. We lay, side by side, her head resting on my arm when we heard a child crying.

"Is that Zach?" I asked.

"No, silly. It's Victor Jr. Can't you tell the difference between a new born baby and a four year old?"

"I guess not," I answered. "But speaking about your own son, are you planning for Zachary to go to Patricia's school? It seems to me it should be perfect for him if they take 'em that young."

"I already asked my daddy, in Texas. He says he'll pay the fees. I'm really excited. I was scared to ask him, what with his paying my own tuition and board for the past three years."

"You're a lucky woman," I said. "Your parents are really there for you."

"Are you surprised, Mark? We're both only children. My parents will do anything for me, and I bet yours are the same way. We've never talked about it, but Daddy's always supported me and Zachary. When I got pregnant, my final term in High school, he insisted that having a baby wasn't going to stop me from going to college. How's that for family!"

"What about the guy who got you pregnant? You've never mentioned him and I never felt it was my business to ask."

"Gone. Disappeared. He doesn't even have a name anymore. We refer to him as the sperm donor."

We cuddled for a bit and then Laura got up, brushed herself clean of loose hay and said, "I'd better get back to my son."

"Please, stay a little longer, Laura. Next week I go to New York for the summer. Who knows how long it will be before we are together again."

"Not now, Mark. I've got an uncomfortable feeling about

Zachary, all alone there. You keep telling me I shouldn't worry, what with so many people here to watch out for him. Don't you? But I do worry when he's alone."

She kissed me, clambered over baled hay and dropped down to the ground, tucked her blouse back into her jeans, straightened her hair, and left me there, lying on my back, wondering how long we could keep up this relationship.

CHAPTER NINETEEN

PEEKSKILL, New York, felt much more homelike in this, my second summer of being what I described as a camp-follower, traipsing after my distant wife, Louella.

I brought Louella pictures of little Victor Junior. She studied them attentively, pleased that her erstwhile friend, Gertrude, was now a mother. But I sensed scarcely hidden concern about when, if ever, her own turn would come.

"Good for her," Louella said. "I'm very happy for her. I hope it works out in the long run."

"What's happened between you two, anyway? She used to be your closest friend. Don't you like her anymore?"

"It isn't that, Mark. Of course I like her. It's just that our lives have gone in completely different directions. She chose Victor, and I chose to have nothing to do with that man. But you know what? Let's go out and find something really nice that we can send them. A friendship token."

By now I had plenty of activity to fill up my vacation, what with reading, hiking, and hours spent in the library preparing new topics to introduce in my teaching next semester. Additionally, I enjoyed meeting and knowing Louella's friends.

I was pleased to see that Louella was keeping up with visits to her father.

"I'm reliable," she said. "Once a month, always on the third Saturday, my Volkswagen takes me fifteen minutes south, to the penitentiary gates."

"So, is he penitent?" I quipped.

"It's not good, Mark. I'm afraid he's defeated, hollow, given up."

"It's that bad?"

"And then some. He's got no job to go back to. His reputation is shot, and I'm not even sure my mother is going to take him back into the house. She'd prefer not to."

"Lousy! I'm sorry for all of you. Are you sure that I'm not allowed to visit?"

"I'm sure."

One evening, early in August, we sat at the supper table, the television playing in the background. We were anticipating the evening news. The McNeil/Lehrer report came on just as the sun was starting to dip below the hills on the opposite bank of the Hudson. The setting sun practically obscuring the image on the ten- inch screen, however, the view out the window was so magnificent we wouldn't even consider putting up venetian blinds or a curtain.

The announcement didn't seem terribly important at the time. Apparently, a North Vietnamese torpedo boat had fired shots at one of our destroyers patrolling in The Gulf of Tonkin. No one was hurt.

Two days later, President Johnson asked for, and got, a "war powers" resolution which essentially gave him the right to do whatever he deemed necessary to protect South Vietnam from the North. In other words, without a declaration of war, he was free to commit U.S. troops into battle.

The resolution was passed unanimously by Congress. Only two Senators opposed it, Wayne Morse and Ernest Gruening. Senator Gruening objected to "sending our boys into combat in a war in which we have no business, which is not our war, into which we have been misguidedly drawn and which is steadily being escalated."

Louella and I agreed with Senator Gruening.

The following morning, seated at the same table, now eating cold cereal, and listening to the radio, we heard that a protest rally was going to be held on the Mall in Washington D.C. on Saturday.

"We should go," I said.

"I'll see if anyone from work will ride down with us."

"Good. You do that, and when you go to work I'll call campus and see if anyone there wants to join us."

Returning home, that afternoon, Louella was disappointed.

"I tried. I talked to everyone with whom I'd be willing to spend five hours, each way, in the car. Everybody agreed with us. Nobody thinks Johnson is right. But nobody wants to go."

"They're afraid," I said. "Afraid they'll lose their jobs."

"You're probably right. Did you phone Ohio? What did you find out?"

"I talked to Al. He says that instead of coming to Washington, they're going to organize a rally on campus. They're inviting students from the other colleges in the area. The Methodists from Wilberforce have already promised to show up. Al says that he and Rita are helping organize it. Most of the people from The Quest will be there, but not Victor. Victor said they could take part in the rally but they shouldn't present themselves as representing The Quest.

The drive down to Washington was exhilarating. It seemed that all the cars crowding the New Jersey Turnpike were heading to the same event, or so we chose to believe. People waved happily as they passed one another, shaking homemade signs out their car windows. The rest stops along the way were packed with young people; long haired boys wore their hair in ponytails; the girls wore flowery, billowing skirts.

When we arrived in Washington the closest parking place we could find was half a mile or so from the Mall. From there we walked, hand in hand, drawn by the other walkers, all heading towards that tall white obelisk, the Washington Monument, which rose above the trees, gleaming white in the sun.

"You know what, Louella? See the way the windows way up top look like two eyes? It kind of makes the whole thing remind you of a hooded Klansman, doesn't it?"

Louella stopped, turned and looked at me quizzically, seriously, "Jeeze, Mark. You shouldn't say that. You shouldn't even think like that. That line of thought is going to get us into trouble."

As we neared the mall, a small group of men stood on the sidewalk holding up signs reading "Better dead than red!" They shouted at us, "If you don't like it here go back to Russia."

I squeezed Louella's hand more tightly. "Well," I said, "for today, at least, we've got them outnumbered." Louella responded by bringing my hand to her lips.

Acres of green lawn surround The Washington Monument. A temporary stage stood to one side. Even before we saw the stage we could hear the folksingers who were entertaining the already large crowd. We made our way to the far edge of the lawn and picked out a spot in the shade of a maple. I spread a blanket which was immediately claimed by an army of small grasshoppers. I set down our picnic sack, brushed away the insects and we settled ourselves on the ground. The stage was too distant for us to recognize faces, but the sound system was powerful and we were comfortable.

There were speeches and there were songs. Prolonged applause greeted the appearance of Pete Seeger, who led us in singing:

Last night I had the strangest dream,
I've never dreamed before,
I dreamed the world had all agreed
to put an end to war.

Among the sea of antiwar signs being waved, the one which particularly made me smile was held up by a scruffy fellow in his thirties. It read, "Fighting for peace is like balling for chastity."

"What do you think, Louella? Is he on our side or isn't he?"

Much later Louella nudged me and pointed to another placard held up by a young woman. It read "Free Charlotte Corday."

"She's kind of late, isn't she?" I said.

"Almost two hundred years. But who's counting?"

The program was nearly over; already people were streaming away from the lawn. A group of Cuban Americans was leading us in "Guantanamera," a song which Pete Seeger had already sung two hours earlier, when a distinct murmur swept through the remaining crowd. It was an oncoming tide, its sound rushing towards us. Before that tide reached Louella and me, one of the leaders walked out onto the stage, took the microphone from the lead singer's hand and said,

"Sorry...I have to interrupt with terrible news. You know we are not alone in protesting Johnson's war. On college campuses all over the country our brothers and sisters are with us, loud and clear, telling Johnson we don't intend to fight his war. Well, I'm afraid, from what we are just hearing, I believe in Illinois or Wisconsin, on a college campus, there has been a shooting. At least two students, it seems, are dead. I wish I could tell you details. That's all I know. Can we have a moment of silence for our fallen comrades."

We stood in silence. The protest rally was finished, although the announcer asked that we all stand up from our spots on the grass, that we all hold hands and that we unite in singing "We shall Overcome."

The mood of the crowd streaming towards their cars and buses was somber, not at all what it had been in the morning. We were tired, of course, but mostly we were sobered by the shooting and waiting to hear particulars.

When we reached Louella's Volkswagen we turned on the radio. As we pulled onto the ramp for the Washington-Baltimore highway we heard that it hadn't been Illinois or Wisconsin after all. The shooting had taken place in Ohio, on our campus, at Horace Mann College.

We drove and we listened. We heard that it wasn't two students who had been shot. Only one of the dead was a student, a freshman from the Methodist school in the next town. The other was a four-year-old infant, brought to the rally by his mother, a student at Horace Mann.

My body twitched as I heard the report. I shuddered. Louella gasped. We looked at each other but said nothing.

A long silence and then I said, "Louella, I'll pull off at the next rest area and call the farm."

"My God!" she said. "It isn't possible. How could it have turned out this way?"

We each were sure; it had to be Laura and Zachary, but neither of us was willing to say it until we heard more on the radio. At the first rest stop there was such a crowd lined up in front of the pay phones that I didn't even try to wait my turn to make a call.

We drove on, mostly in silence, listening to the radio. Just north of the Philadelphia spur we stopped again and I waited in a shorter line for my turn to call the farm. I got a busy signal. On my fifth try I got through.

It was Victor who answered the phone.

"Yes, it's all true," he said. "Hannah has been with Laura ever since the rescue squad brought her here, to us. Hannah is going to accompany her back to Texas. to her parents' home. She'll stay with her until after the funeral. In fact they are getting ready to go to the airport now. Zachary's body will be flown on the same plane. Laura won't be coming back, and Mark, you shouldn't try to follow her."

"What do you mean, 'I shouldn't follow?'"

"You know what I mean, Mark. Did you think that I didn't know. I'm awake. I pay attention. That's what you're learning to do, I hope. Anyway, there isn't anything that you can do for her. You are to stay with Louella."

I conveyed only the first part of Victor's message to my wife. We got back onto the highway and listened to the radio as the story gradually unfolded.

"Hannah is such a good person," Louella said. "I hardly know Laura, but it's comforting to know that Hannah is there for her."

I didn't respond. What I was feeling was horror, but also in my mind there was an odd sense of peace. Clearly, this tragedy meant the end of my involvement in a guilt producing, hidden relationship.

You have no right to even think such thoughts, Mark! But the idea had already come, unbidden.

We drove on. By now the radio had begun to tell a coherent story.

We heard that the rally had started out peacefully. The scene was described; a stage had been set up in front of the main building, a courtyard which we knew well. The broadcaster went on to set the scene, describing the brick edifice, one-hundred years old, and dominated by two massive towers, each capped with a slate roof.

"Enough, already," I shouted. "We know what it looks like. What happened?"

We were told that two large American flags stood on either side of the hastily built stage. Faculty members spoke on the history of the Vietnamese conflict, explaining how America had now taken up the burden of defeating the insurgency that the French were unable to control. Several students spoke of their unwillingness to go and fight "Johnson's war".

The radio identified one of those students, Calvin Hollister. I knew him to be the older brother of a girl who had been in my class at The Lab School. Calvin, in the midst of a professor's speech, strode to the microphone, took out his wallet, extracted his draft card and, with a cigarette lighter, set the card afire. He urged others to come up onto the stage and do likewise. A few of the students responded, climbing onto the stage and in turn burning their draft cards. The applause from the crowd grew, and as it increased in volume increasingly more young men clambered up and took out their draft cards.

In the frenzy of the moment one of the draft card burners walked to the side of the stage where an American flag was attached to a wooden flagpole. He held up an end of the flag and tried to ignite it from his flaming draft card. The cloth was slow to ignite, but as others saw what he was doing, they too came, bringing additional flame to bear. Soon the flag was a mass of flames.

Providing "security" for the rally, county officials had made sure that the local police would be backed up by sheriff's patrol and armed officers from surrounding towns. Also, there was a contingent of volunteer firemen holding up a large American flag of their own as well as a banner that read "America. Love it or leave it."

Seeing the American flag go up in flames, the protectors of

order rushed the stage. At the same time somebody set off a gas canister.

Responding to the oncoming officers and firemen, several students picked up chairs and used them as weapons to drive back the attackers. Shots, perhaps warning shots, were fired into the air.

But not all the shots were fired into the air. A piercing scream was heard. Both sides paused.

The momentary silence was pierced by the wailing siren of the campus ambulance which had been standing by.

There were two deaths: a freshman from a neighboring school and an infant. Names of the deceased were still being withheld, but by the time we reached New York State the news broadcasts were saying that the unwed mother and her deceased infant had been living in a "new age" commune close to the campus. The child, at the time of the shooting, had been held in his mother's arms.

We reached Louella's apartment and immediately turned on the television. There was Jeremy, in the farm dining room, his pudginess further puffed up and emphasized by his obvious pleasure at finding himself in front of television cameras, telling the nation what a sweet child Zachary had been.

CHAPTER TWENTY

PHYSICALLY EXHAUSTED and emotionally drained, we went to bed without any further discussion and fell asleep immediately.

In the morning I popped out of bed and went right back to the television. When Louella came into the living room wearing pajamas and a light bathrobe I already had the coffee brewing.

"Is there anything new?" she asked.

"Nothing important. They keep repeating the same things, over and over again. Listen, Louella, I've got three weeks left in my summer vacation, but I've been thinking. I can't justify sitting here in The Hudson Valley while everything at Cold Springs is falling apart. Everything there has to be completely changed now. I've got to go back and find out where I fit in—what my part is supposed to be."

Louella's attention was divided between my announcement and the scene on the television screen. After a pause she asked, "What do you mean by completely changed?"

"Well, for one thing, it's going to be an awful lot of years before anyone, anywhere, is going to hear the name of Horace Mann College without jumping straight to yesterday's horror."

We paused again to take in a repeat of last night's interview at the farm.

"Yes. That's true. Things won't be exactly the same, will they?"

"So what do you think, Louella. You can see why I need to go back right away, can't you?"

"You've got to decide, Mark. I can't decide for you. But sure, if you think that you can be of any use, then that's where you belong."

I wanted to be of use to my college, but also I wanted to be of use to Laura.

*

Two days later I was back on campus and I'd already figured out what I could contribute.

Monday morning I went straight to the Administration Building, the same Victorian brick edifice which was now familiar to the whole country. I went to see my friend, Tom Lacy, who was no longer head of the Psychology Department. He had been promoted to Dean of the College. Tom still thought that I walked on water. He'd thought so ever since, as he often told people, "Mark transformed my son, Bobby from a lout into a voracious reader who's now a model student."

I didn't deserve the credit but I'd long since given up trying to convince Tom that it wasn't my doing; Bobby simply had got himself to the point where he was ready to read.

I went to see Tom in his new office. Opening the heavy oak door marked "Dean of the College" and walking in, I was reminded how large and forceful Tom was. At the same time, I was pleased that he no longer intimidated me.

Tom was seated behind a large desk strewn with papers. He looked up, recognized me, and smiled broadly.

Swiveling my head and taking in the full expanse of the oak paneled office, I said, "Not bad! Not bad at all!"

"Yes. It's an improvement. It's a big step up from my cubby hole in the Psych. Department. Tom rose from behind his desk and motioned that we sit in the leather easy chairs on the other side of the room.

"Good to see you again, Mark. We've missed you at volleyball. Well, we missed you until all hell broke loose here. We don't think about volleyball any more. You picked a funny time to be off campus. Now you're back but it's not the same place you left. Never will be. You know that, don't you?"

"Yeah, that's sort of what I expected I'd be coming back to. Actually it's why I'm back early."

We each sighed and were silent for a moment. I took a deep breath.

"You know what brings me here. What else is there anymore? It's Laura Steiner, Tom. Did you ever meet her?"

"No, Poor girl, I don't think I ever did."

"Well, she's a full year from graduating—or she was, a full year from graduating. I'm sure you've already figured out that she won't be coming back for her final year."

"The last thing in the world that girl needs is to spend any more time here, on campus." Tom said.

"Right, Tom. You know, don't you, that I'm involved with Victor Lamotta's group. They call it The Quest, out at the old Otto Mays farm, where Laura Steiner had been living. I know her well."

"Yes, I've heard."

What has he heard? I wondered. *Victor knew about me and Laura. Did the whole world know? Doesn't matter! I'll say my say. Tom will take it or leave it.*

"Well, here's my thought. Maybe two thoughts. First of all we owe it to her to give her support—help. Somebody from the college has to remain in touch with her. Second thought. From now on, way into the future, Laura's name and our college's name are linked. So what do we tell the world? We have to acknowledge the link. If nothing else It seems to me we have to find a way that she can gradu-ate. She didn't ask for this, but her name is going down in the history books. So why don't we make the most of it? Maybe we ask Laura to do a senior thesis, to chronicle the whole experience. It will be good for her to put her thoughts down on paper. And whatever she comes up with is automatically an historical document, to be archived and be treasured."

"You mean she writes the paper and we grant her the degree, without her coming back to campus?"

"That's exactly what I mean. I don't know how she's going to feel about the whole idea, after having her child blown away, right in her arms, but I feel that we owe it to her to make the offer."

When I finished Tom closed his eyes and was silent for a

moment. Then he looked at me and said "You are certainly right when you say that we cannot simply leave her to herself."

He sat up, with his fingers intertwined. Then he unfolded his body from the depths of his easy chair, stood, and came behind my chair. He put his large hands onto my shoulders and said, "You are onto something, Mark, and I'll tell you why. You have realized that Horace Mann College has been tainted forever. There isn't a person in America who hears the name of our school and doesn't immediately see students being shot at. It's going to be that way for as long as any of us are still here."

Removing his hands from my shoulders and returning to his seat Tom continued. "Seems to me that the only thing left for us to do is to embrace this as part of our history and try to make something of it. Honoring Laura Steiner might well be our first step towards redemption. And yes, you are right. Somebody needs to remain in touch with her. Seems to me, you've come up with something good."

I felt a warm surge of satisfaction at the dean's approval. Yes! I do have a role here.

"One more thing," he said. "Finding the right faculty member to work with her is going to be vital. Have you thought about who it should be?"

"No, I haven't," I lied." I hadn't intended to lie. But it came out that way.

"Well maybe you should be the one to handle it."

"Me? I'm an instructor in the education department I don't qualify as a thesis advisor."

"No. Not now, you don't," Tom answered. "It's true. We tend to forget you guys sitting way out there in the Lab School. So you're still an instructor, are you? After how many years? But suppose we make you an assistant professor and put you down as a part-time associate in the History Department. I think I can push it through with no trouble. We're a small school, Mark, and we all know each other. You figure out how to sell the idea to Laura Steiner. I'll sell it to the rest of the administration."

"I'm overwhelmed," I said.

"Nah. You've earned the promotion. Everyone knows what a good job you're doing out there." Tom patted me on the back, stood, and returned to his desk, where he opened his calendar and penciled in something.

"How about you come back next Wednesday, say at eleven? By then we'll see how far we can push this."

Clearly it was time to go. I rose, thanked Tom, and asked him to give my best wishes to his son Bobby. As I left the Administration Building, for the first time in my life I understood the expression "to walk on air."

Too excited to wait until the afternoon, I called Louella at work and told her about my conversation with the dean.

"Mark, I'm so proud of you!" she said.

"Well, it hasn't happened yet, so let's not get too excited."

"Of course you can be excited. It's okay," Louella said. "The problem will be persuading Laura Steiner to go along with the idea. I don't think she'll want to have anything to do with anything that reminds her of Horace Mann College."

"Right," I said.

"But you know what? It sounds to me as though Tom Lacy has committed himself to your future. I don't think he'll turn his back on you, no matter what Laura decides."

"From your mouth, to God's ear," I replied.

At this moment I was feeling doubly pleased; pleased with what seemed to be my new status at the college, and pleased that Louella appeared to have no inkling of suspicion that I was anything but an acquaintance of Laura Steiner's.

"Mark, here's what you need to do. Before you do anything else, you've got to go out to the farm and talk to Hannah, the minute she gets back from Texas. She isn't back already, is she?"

"No. Zachary's funeral was yesterday."

"I know. I watched. Just like everybody else."

"I know you did."

"Anyway, don't do anything without Hannah's advice. She'll know Laura's feeling. Go see Hannah and listen to her. Do what she tells you to do!"

CHAPTER TWENTY-ONE

IT WAS another week before Hannah got back from Texas: a week of impatience. On the day she returned, when my school day was over I went right out to the farm, expecting there would be plenty of time to present my proposal to Hannah, and still have supper there before my evening session with Victor.

When I arrived, there was Gertrude, rocking on the front porch, nursing her month old son, whom I hadn't yet met. Seeing me, Gertrude said, "What do you think of Victor Jr., Mark?"

"He's beautiful, I think. As much as I can see of him, he takes after both of you."

"You're a bullshitter, aren't you Mark?"

I smiled, enjoying the sound of Victor Jr.'s noisy sucking.

"Well, you two do look marvelous, Gertrude. What's it like being a mother?"

"Nothing's wrong with it that a little sleep wouldn't cure," she said.

"What about Victor?" I asked. "Is he doing his share or should I give him a talking to?"

"Hah!" she replied. "You think he'd listen to you? You've got a class with him tonight, don't you? Well, this has been a red-letter day for Victor and he'll probably spend half of the session bragging about it. Today, for the first time, he actually changed little Vickie's diaper. Once!"

"See," I said, kissing Gertrude on the cheek. "See, step by step, life is getting easier, after all." Saying that, I left her and went into the farm house.

Not finding Hannah downstairs, I went upstairs and knocked on her door.

"Who is it?"

"It's me, Mark. Can I come in?"

"Of course you may, Mark." She emphasized the word 'may'.

I entered. Hannah remained seated in an armchair. I bent to kiss her, surprised at how white her curly hair had become.

This was my first time in Hannah's room. The large bedroom was now the only remaining part of Hannah's farmhouse that was still distinctly hers. It was crammed with Victorian oak furnishings, rescued from downstairs. Tall bookshelves held Hannah's personal books, most in German, which she had brought upstairs when her library was converted to communal dining space. Heavy green curtains blocked out most of the remaining daylight. A bedside lamp was the only illumination.

"Sit down. Tell me all about your summer in New York. Tell me how your wife is doing out there."

I lowered myself into one of the stuffed armchairs, Hannah remained opposite me in the other.

"No," I said. "First, you tell me. You just got back from Texas. It must have been a hard time for you. Harder for Laura, of course, but hard on you too. How was it?"

"Yes, of course, it was horrible. But it was so good that I went. Good for Laura, but good for me too."

"How do you mean, Hannah?"

"Have you tried to imagine what that girl went through? Her child was shot to death while she carried him in her arms! Don't try. There is no way you could know. But we talked and we talked and I was of some help because I do know. Mark, you and I never discussed my past, in Germany, did we?"

"No. I hadn't any right to open up that subject."

"True. But now I'll tell you so you'll understand what went on in Texas. You see, Otto wasn't my first husband. Maybe you knew that?"

"No, I didn't."

"Otto and I met in America, after the war. Before the war I was married to Aaron, a teacher in the Gymnasium. We were married in

1932. We lived in Berlin. Two years later our daughter, Rivka, was born. Rivka was six years old when we were rounded up and shipped by train to Dachau. You've seen my tattooed arm, of course, but you never asked about it. Why was that, Mark?"

"What can I say?... I was afraid to ask. It wasn't my place to ask."

"And it wasn't my job to tell you. But now I'm telling you. When we got to Dachau my Aaron was separated from us. I never saw him again. The following day I was assigned to a work brigade, shoveling coal. All day long Rivka would be alone, in the care of nobody in particular, just whoever happened to notice her. Somehow it worked out for the first week. Then a new order came. All the children were taken from us. Is my daughter still alive? She would be thirty-two years old now. Older than you are. Two years older. I have no reason to think that she lives."

"My God, Hannah," I said, reaching across to take her hand.

She withdrew her hand, saying, "I don't have any more tears for my daughter, nor for myself. I didn't even have any tears for Laura. But I think that Laura was able to listen to me and to feel a little bit less abandoned in this cruel world. Perhaps she drew some comfort in seeing that life does go on, somehow."

"All this time I've considered you my close friend, Hannah, and I've known absolutely nothing about your past. I'm ashamed that I never asked, or even wondered."

"That's right, Mark. You go through life with blinders on. Or, as Victor says, in a state of sleep."

"But," she continued, "I suspect that you came to my room for something more than just saying hello. Was it to find out how Laura is doing, or is there something else on your mind?"

"You're right, sort of. I did come to talk about Laura."

I proceeded to lay out my plan for having Laura earn her degree without having to return to school. I spoke of my meeting with Dean Lacy and of how pleased I was to be the one assigned to be Laura's thesis advisor.

"That's the plan." I said. "Louella advised me to discuss it with you. She said you'd know the best way to make it happen.—No, that's not exactly what she said. She said that you would be the right person to present the idea to Laura, that she might be able to hear it from you, if not from anyone else."

"A wise woman, your wife," Hannah said. "But first let's talk about why you want to do this. Laura and I spoke of just about everything while I was in Texas. As you might suppose, Laura spoke about you too. About you and her, that is. I'll admit, I had no suspicion. I was shocked."

Hannah paused for a moment, looking into my eyes. Her stare was questioning, more than accusing. Nonetheless, I felt myself diminished, squirming in my armchair.

Hannah continued, "Although, being there with Laura,—after what she's gone through—there's very little left to shock me anymore. What you two have done was wrong, Mark. If now, you are proposing this so that you can still make love to Laura, then I think it isn't a good thing. It would be vile, horrible, disgusting!"

"No." I answered, upset that Laura had spoken of our affair. I was angry. Then, censoring my thoughts, it was clear that poor Laura's need to speak was greater than any rights I might have in the matter.

"It isn't that at all. When I went to Dean Lacy with my suggestion I certainly didn't think that I could be picked to be her thesis advisor. True....I wanted it to be me, but it was Dean Lacy who made the suggestion. Not me."

Even as I said these words I was less sure of my motives. Perhaps, somewhere in the back of my mind, there has lurked the hope that this senior thesis scheme was a pretext for my being with Laura. Aloud, I continued to deny that this was my intention, but I was less than sure that I was being truthful.

Hannah sat silently for a moment and then said, "Well, it certainly would be a good thing for Laura to graduate. There isn't much good that can come from staying at home with her parents. But I don't think that you should be the one to work with her. Give me a day to think about it. If I decide that it's proper for you to do this, then tomorrow night I'll telephone Laura and try to talk her into doing it."

I stood.

"Thank you Hannah." I reached down and held both her hands. "Thank you for letting me into your past. And thank you for being so wise. Now let's go downstairs to supper."

"No. You go, Mark. I don't feel like eating communally tonight. Later I'll go down and prepare myself something. Maybe I'll bring it up here."

"You're coming to our group's class with Victor, after supper, aren't you?"

"No. You go. I think I've had enough of Victor's wisdom for a while."

CHAPTER TWENTY-TWO

I LEFT Hannah to her chosen solitude and returned downstairs to join Victor and nine of his followers at the supper table. Gertrude and her newborn son were elsewhere.

We ate, and then the five of us in Victor's "more-advanced" group followed him out to the barn, leaving the others to wash the dishes.

We now met downstairs, in one of the newly completed class-rooms: in the space where, before Dr. Otto Mays' death, his black Angus herd had been stalled. There were eight of us in attendance. We were the "old timers." Jeremy and Patricia, Al and Rita, and I made up the core of the group. Three others who were already seated had been in the group back when Louella first dragged me there but their level of participation in the group life at the farm was minimal. Laura Steiner had been a member of our class. So was Hannah, and I hoped that Hannah's decision not to attend tonight was only a temporary reaction to the upheaval that had sent her to Texas, to accompany and to comfort poor Laura.

The eight of us sat on straight-backed wooden chairs. Victor, in a taller, padded chair, faced us.

Looking smug, grinning, he peered from face to face and said, "This has been a big day in my family. I bonded with my little son, Victor Jr. He let me change his diapers and I could tell he loved having me do it."

He sighed and the smile morphed into a serious expression.

"But that's not what we're here to talk about, is it? Let's get to work."

"First, you'll connect with your bodies.... use each of your senses...follow your breath...be aware of your presence... "

We meditated for twenty minutes, then Victor began his talk.

"This is our first meeting since the events on campus, and since Laura has left us for Texas and gone back to her parents. Tonight I want to suggest how you might regard these events."

"You already know that it's all about energy. We are here, on this planet, on this 'ray of creation', to serve in the process of conscious evolution. You've understood, by now, that we use energy, either consciously or unconsciously. We get the grossest kind of energy from the food we eat. This energy can be assimilated without conscious attention. Finer energy is assimilated through our senses, through awareness. Likewise, the planet is constantly consuming and adjusting its energy consumption. The finest kind of energy is released when something alive becomes dead. This energy, as it is released, is utilized in the planet's creative evolution. At times the planet demands more energy and then wars break out. The energy released by the two deaths, here on campus, fed the process of creation."

Victor stood up, looked at us and asked, "Was that difficult for you to accept?" He turned to the blackboard and wrote the words "personality" and "essence."

"I'll tell you why, at first, it is hard for you to accept this: why your ideas get in the way."

He returned to his chair.

"You all have grown up with ideas that have been fed to you, ideas which you will swear are true. You are full of ideas and none of them are true.

That's what we mean when we talk about personality, Your ideas have been assimilated, obscuring your essence. It is 'personality' which looks at transitory events and assigns them false importance. Your essence is to participate in a world that is perfect. You are a part of that perfection.

You can either try to change the world according to the transitory dictates of your personality, or you can change yourself by waking up."

Unwinding his lean frame, Victor returned to the blackboard, picked up the chalk and drew an X through the word personality.

Rapping his knuckles on the blackboard, he said "This is the task facing you. To replace personality with essence."

He returned to his chair, smiled, and asked "How many of you have read *War and Peace*?"

Patricia and I were the only ones to raise our hands.

"Shame on the rest of you." Victor said. "Read it."

"Leo Tolstoi's great book concludes with not one, but with two epilogues, and the second epilogue has driven critics to distraction. It isn't part of the story. It is an attempt to derive the natural laws that governed the "unthinking" movements of immense armies, first driving them towards the east, and then pulling them in the opposite direction, west. Tolstoi's great intellect told him that natural laws demanded these bloody migrations. But he, and his readers as well, are tormented by his inability to grasp these laws. All he was able to conclude was, in his own words, that "...it is necessary to renounce a freedom that does not exist, (he meant 'free will') and to recognize a dependence of which we are not conscious."

I saw, from Victor's brightly shining eyes that he was thrilled to be drawing on the works of the master, Tolstoi, to illuminate the teachings of his own guru, Gurdjief.

"Tolstoi came close." Victor continued, "Remember, as a youth he took part in the Tsar's military expeditions into the Caucuses, the very place from which Gurdjief began his quest for esoteric knowledge. Tolstoi was sure that there must be laws governing the bloodletting that convulsed Europe; he just didn't know what those laws were."

Victor again stood, tall and straight. He brushed back loose strands of hair on the sides of his otherwise bald head and for a moment he stood there, looking at each of us.

"I've unlocked the mystery for you." Victor concluded. "It isn't easy to make the turn; to see everything from a completely new perspective. But it's necessary. Just remember, these lessons are not to be taken on faith. Try them out. See if they make sense."

I wanted to understand Victor's message. Before going to sleep, lying in my bed, I telephoned my wife, thinking if I could convey the ideas to her, that would probably mean that I had grasped them.

I told her, "Victor talked about death in a completely new way. He explained death as a release of energy, into the universe... No, not just a release...sort of a repossession...the universe taking back something that it needs. Weird! But then he went in a different direction. He implied that every one of the ideas we hold true, ideas about life and death, are part of our false personality; notions we've picked up that aren't true at all. It's a tall order, accepting all of this, Louella."

Her response, crisply heard in the darkness of my bedroom, from six-hundred miles away, was disappointing.

"Well," she said, "So that's how he wants you to think about little Zachary's death, is it? I'm glad that you want to share your confusion with me, but don't expect sympathy. You know what I think of his ideas, don't you?"

"Yeah. Let's not go there tonight. Mostly just thanks for listening. I'm going to sleep."

I spent the next day preparing my own classroom for the opening of school, which was still a week away. The following evening Hannah called to report on her telephone call to Laura.

"So? Does she like the idea? Will she write the senior thesis? Will she let me be her advisor?"

"No. She wont. She won't even think about it. She isn't able to think about anything beyond hcr miscry."

I was acutely disappointed. An entire future, which I had been building in my imagination, dropped away and I felt a void inside of me where that imagined future had been lodged.

"That's not pleasant news," I said. "Did you try to persuade her that this would be good for her?"

"Don't be foolish, Mark."

"But suppose we don't give up so easily. How about I try to present the idea myself? Do you think she'll listen to me?"

"Don't you dare, Mark. I forbid you to have anything more to do with that poor girl. It's over!"

*

What am I going to tell Dean Lacy? This is going to destroy his faith in me, won't it? So much for all his promises of advancing my career.

Unsure, I did nothing; I spent most of the day in the college library, brooding on my bad luck.

The next afternoon Hannah phoned me again.

"Mark," she said, "are you free? May I come over? We need to talk in person. I'll be right there."

While waiting I mixed us iced tea. I rummaged in the pantry until I found a box of cookies which I opened and put onto a plate. I brought the refreshments outside to the patio behind our house, where we kept two wooden Adirondack chairs.

Hannah arrived in her bright-yellow Toyota pick up truck, a reminder that before Otto's death the two of them had actively farmed their property.

She sat down and immediately told me her news.

"I've been on the telephone with Laura, on and off, for the entire day. It's madness there. Apparently, it's taken this long for the press to locate her. Yesterday the Chicago Tribune did a long story about her, telling the world where Laura is living with her parents, and now, she says, "The jackals won't leave me for a second." They want interviews. They want her to be on television. Agents are asking for the exclusive right to manage her story. Then there are the "patriots" on the other side. Somebody put up a sign outside the house, reading "Your kid was shot because he's a commie." And that's not all. The 'low life' who fathered Zachary turned up, for the first time in four years, saying he wants to be part of the action."

"She doesn't know what to do. Her father is furious at all the intrusion but, Laura says, he is no help at all. She wants you to come out there, right away, to save her, to take care of her, or at least to advise her."

"Hannah." I said, "You told me all of that without pausing for one breath. Slow down, drink some tea and let's think.

We drank. I ate a cookie. Hannah didn't. And then I said, "Of course I'll go. I can go tomorrow. School doesn't start till Monday. You know what? I don't know where she lives in Texas. Somewhere near Houston? I've never been to Texas. I don't even know the telephone number out there. But you'll tell me all that."

"Thank you Mark. I believe that you'll protect her. You'll have to figure out for yourself what's the right thing to do."

Using two arms to push herself upright from the chair Hannah came over to me, bent down and kissed me on the forehead. Then she returned to her seat, refilled her glass and sat for a few moments. Silently, she began sipping her drink.

"There's something else on your mind, Hannah. Isn't there? What is it?

"Not now. You've got enough to deal with."

"No. Tell me."

"It's just that I'm not very happy any more, Mark. We'll talk about me another time."

CHAPTER TWENTY-THREE

WHEN SHE returned to the farm, Hannah must have told somebody I would be meeting with Laura in Dallas because later in the evening, when my phone rang and I picked up the receiver, there was Victor.

"Hello Mark, this is Victor."

"Yes, I know your voice, Victor."

"Listen. You mustn't go to Texas tomorrow. I have a strong premonition that it's wrong for you."

"What do you mean, Victor? I've got to go. I can't back out just because you have a feeling."

"It's more than a feeling, Mark; a certainty. I see something terrible happening to you. Don't go!"

"You're kidding me, aren't you? This is crazy."

"Listen. I don't want you to go, Mark."

"Thanks for the warning. But Laura is expecting me. I'm going. Goodbye, Victor."

I hung up the phone and wondered, *Is he trying to assert his dominance over me, to control me, to show that he's the alpha male? I've seen him do that sort of thing with his students, more than once.*

In the morning I met with the dean, Tom Lacy. I told him that Laura's acceptance of my tutorial help had been denied, but that she now needed my help in simply coping. "Maybe she is changing her mind. I have no idea what she has in mind. We will see." And that afternoon, courtesy of Horace Mann College, I was aboard a TWA flight from Cincinnati to Dallas.

Laura, driving her father's Town Car, picked me up at the airport. When I saw her I recalled the first time I met her: the tall, student with long black hair, working next to me, down on her hands and knees, polishing the floor in the church annex. I remembered the exciting view of her exposed bosom. Now she looked thinner. The long black hair was stringy, unkempt. Her face was pale and she wore no make-up. She tried to smile. We hugged and she was a rag-doll in my arms.

"You drive, Mark. I'll tell you how to go."

It was a grander car than any I had ever driven, but once I got it into motion my attention returned to Laura's appearance: smaller than I'd remember and seemingly doing her best to scrunch down, to disappear into the plush upholstery of her father's auto.

We spoke very little during the thirty minute drive to their suburban development. A television truck was parked in front of the split-level ranch home. Without commenting on the intruders, Laura unfolded her body, reached up to push a button on the visor, the garage door rose and we drove in.

Laura introduced me to her mother and father who thanked me for coming and then hastily left us alone in the living room. We sank into an overstuffed couch facing a large wooden television cabinet, the doors of which were closed and on top of which sat a framed photograph of four-year-old Zachary grinning up from his tricycle, parked in the driveway of his grandparents' house. Next to the couch stood her father's gun cabinet.

"That's a powerful arsenal you guys have here," I said.

"When I was in high school Daddy used to take me hunting. I'm not a bad shot." Then Laura's face paled and she began crying.

I held her for a short while, until the sobbing stopped.

"I'm sorry Laura. I didn't mean to bring you to that place. But you're probably there all of the time anyway. So let's talk about how you're going to go on from here."

We spoke for hours, not once mentioning our past relationship, although it was very much on my mind. Clearly, it was not going to be renewed, and after a while I realized how relieved I was that all desire for sexual intimacy was fully gone... well, if not gone, at least I knew such desire wasn't going to be acted upon. I spent two nights at the Steiner's home.

We talked late into that first night. I told her about my conversations with Dean Lacy and about the plans I was making for her.

It wasn't hard to convince Laura to keep a written record of what was happening. "Whether it's for me," she said, "or for poor Zachary. In any case, it may do some good."

We even made some plans for the next day; a start on her organizing a new life.

When I emerged from the guest room in the morning Laura had breakfast ready for me.

"How did you sleep?" she asked.

"Fine, thanks, but you look like you've been up the whole night."

"I haven't had a proper night's sleep since it happened."

That morning we boxed all of Zachary's clothes and toys, put them into the Town Car, along with his tricycle, and took it all to the Salvation Army thrift shop.

Returning from our expedition, we saw that the television and radio news crews were back again. Furthermore, the quiet residential street now had an incessant parade of curious gawkers, slowly driving past the house. Again, we did our best to ignore them.

Laura's parents fed us and sat with us at meals. Otherwise they left us alone. It appeared to me they were overwhelmed, unable to cope and were hoping that somehow I would be able to deliver their daughter, and perhaps themselves as well, from the turmoil that had taken possession of their previously tranquil life.

As we had done the day before, we spoke incessantly. Laura told me about her privileged childhood as the daughter of one of the city's prominent auto dealers, about becoming pregnant in her senior year of high school, and about her choice of Horace Mann College as the only place she could find that was liberal enough to accept her as a freshman, accompanied by her infant.

Our conversation kept circling around the events of the war, the war protestors, and then back to the shooting on campus. We speculated on what was coming, on what role Laura would have in upcoming events. I kept reminding her that she was no longer simply Laura Steiner.

"Now you are Laura Steiner, the mother of the late Zachary Steiner, the child who was shot dead as she held him in her arms. There isn't anybody in this country who doesn't know who you are—hardly anybody in the world."

We talked. Sometimes Laura cried, but mostly she expressed wonder at what was happening and determination to make something good come of it. Gradually she, or possibly we together, came to the realization of how much Laura had to offer: that her words would be listened to and that they carried weight.

"Mark," she said, "Now I'm a part of the fight. Who better than me to tell Johnson to get us out of Viet Nam," she said. "At least then I can see that Zachary's death will have had some kind of significance. Without that, if it was just meaningless, I couldn't go on with my life—not if it's all for nothing."

Sunday morning Laura drove me back to the airport. She found an empty spot by the "departures" platform. We both exited the car, stood and embraced.

"Be strong," I said. "Two weeks. In just two weeks I'll be back. Meanwhile, I promise, we'll talk on the telephone every night."

CHAPTER TWENTY-FOUR

AS PROMISED I did speak to Laura every night. Clearly, my telephone calls were important to her.

"These calls are all that's keeping me sane," Laura told me.

"I'm glad to hear you're staying sane," I replied, "but are you doing everything we said? Are you writing down your thoughts, and not just unburdening yourself onto my shoulders?"

"Of course I am. The journal is my reason for getting out of bed in the morning, writing it and having your assurance that something important is going to come of it."

That's when I realized that I'd better keep a diary too. I began it that night.

The following night I surprised myself. After the evening's task of holding Laura's hand, over the telephone, so to speak, I'd started to replace the phone on its receiver when, without any conscious intent, I found myself dialing Louella's number.

"How is it going?" was her first question. "Is she still working on her paper for you?"

"Yes. I think so. This whole thing is going to be much more complicated than I thought."

"How so?"

"Listen, Louella, this long distance communication stinks. I need to look at you, to see your face."

"I'm not following you. What's suddenly different?"

"It's just that I've got too much going around in my head now and I need to see you. Either you come home this weekend, or I'll fly out to you, but I do need to see you in person. Not on the phone."

"Such a mystery! Look, if you can't even give me a hint of what it is that you need to talk about, I'm not sure how I'll hold out, even till the weekend. What do you want to happen? Tell me."

"No. It will wait till the weekend. There's school all week and then I'll fly out to White Plains airport, Saturday morning. Our regular flight. You'll pick me up Saturday morning. OK?"

The first day of school was all pleasure. The children appeared happy to be back. So was I. Tuesday night Louella called.

"Cancel your plane tickets," She said. "I've enough vacation time saved up and it turns out that I can be spared for a whole week. I'll be home Friday night!"

"Stupendous! Thanks sweetheart. I'm so glad." Friday evening I met Louella at the airport. As she walked up the ramp toward me I saw her carefully removing her white gloves. They were in her pocketbook by the time she reached me and we kissed.

As we left the short term parking lot Louella said, "OK, now you can tell me what's happening."

"There's so much to catch up on," I said, "and it hasn't been that long, has it? Best news, Laura is cooperating, senior thesis and all. And I'm going to be her advisor. But it isn't as simple as it sounds. I'm not just advising on her thesis. She's become a celebrity and, apparently, I'm her agent. She wants me to help her decide what interviews she'll give, what journals she'll write for, what speaking engagements she should accept. Meanwhile she'll keep a journal. It'll be part diary, and part exploration of her emotions, an attempt to understand what this all means. The journal is going to be the basis of her thesis."

"I see what you mean by complicated," Louella said. "You and your movie star!"

"And there's more. Much more. There's a whole new relationship between me and the college. I've got my promotion, but it means they'll expect all kinds of things from me. Things they never asked for before."

"Like what?"

"Like they'll be watching me all the time. Committees, meetings, oh, and starting next spring, teaching at least one section in the education sequence."

We'd almost reached homewhen I realized the conversation had all been about me so far.

"We haven't talked about your job at all, Louella. Tell me how it's going," I asked, as if I could hope to understand anything about what she actually did there.

She tried to tell me.

"Are you still working with Joe Rizzo?", I asked.

"Mark, you're going to make me think you're actually jealous."

"You're teasing, aren't you?"

Louella didn't answer me. The last few minutes we drove in silence, watching the fast fading twilight.

Once home, I opened a bottle of Chianti and we sat together on the couch. I poured. Louella sipped her wine and said, "There's something else that you want to tell me, Mark. I'm sure there is."

"Yes. And I'm not sure how to begin, but here goes."

I let the words come out without editing or censoring.

"I dreamed up this project. Didn't I? It's big, and if I don't clarify things, I'm sure I'll botch it up. It's about our marriage too. And it's about my relationship with Laura Steiner."

"First about us. I think that we have a good marriage. Sure, it's an odd living arrangement but I know we love each other and I know that there isn't anybody else that I'd want to live with. Not for a moment."

Louella listened carefully, sitting straight and perfectly still, holding her nearly full wine glass and with her eyes locked on mine.

"But I need to tell you... somehow I got involved with Laura. It isn't love. It never was love. It was sex. It happened. It's over. I just came back from spending two nights in her home in Texas and I know it's over. But it happened, and now it looks like I'm going to be spending lots of time working with her this year. I had to tell you. I don't think I could go on pretending it didn't happen. Hannah knows. Laura told her, and somehow Victor figured it out himself."

Louella remained absolutely still until I finished speaking, then she flung what remained of her Chianti into my face.

"You son of a bitch! You're a bastard! Why are you telling me this? What do you want from me?" Then she began to cry.

I took a handkerchief from my pocket and mopped my face. I felt completely hollow, as if there was nothing left of me.

"I guess this means that you and Joe Rizzo weren't having an affair out there. That was just my imagination."

Sniffling and holding back tears Louella said, "Go ahead. Make it worse. You really are a terrible person."

"I don't want to be a terrible person, Louella. I'm telling you all this because I want to make a new start. No more lying."

I reached across to take her hand. She threw my hand back towards my lap.

"How long has this been going on?"

"It started when you were off studying for your Master's in Columbus."

"I have no idea why you told me this, Mark. But I know that I don't want to talk to you now and I'm going to bed, and I don't want you to follow me. You sleep on the couch and tomorrow...."

Louella got up without finishing her sentence, went down the hallway and slammed the bedroom door.

I remained, for a long time, unmoving, sitting in the same chair, trying to understand what I had just done. There had to have been a reason why it had seemed right to unburden myself. Why? Then I knew.

I know why I told her. I told her so that it would be impossible to go back and make love to Laura, ever again. I'd feel that Louella was watching over my shoulder, so to speak. Was it fair to have done this? She's right, of course. I hurt her terribly and it was just to make my life easier. Now what?

*

In the morning I was awakened by my wife's voice, calling me from the bedroom. I was surprised to find myself on the couch and then remembered why I was there. Strange, I thought, how soundly I slept.

"Mark. Come in here please."

Still in yesterday's underwear, I stood up and went to her.

"Come to bed. Lie down next to me." she said, lifting up a corner of the bedding.

I lay down as instructed, unsure of what was happening but pleased to be back in our bed. I lay on my back. She turned away from me. I turned towards her, putting my arms around her and we lay like spoons.

"You're a selfish man." she said. "You're hardly a man. You're a spoiled brat who wants it all. You didn't tell me all that to make me feel good. It was all for your own sake that you told me. But you're what I've got. Somehow we'll make a go of it."

At noon Louella and Hannah Mays met for lunch at the diner. When she returned home I was on the patio, sipping a cold beer and enjoying the surrounding greenery. In fact, I was practicing Victor's teachings; I consciously noted my presence, became aware that I was looking at the varying hues of green: some bright in the sun, others dark in the shade. I took pleasure in the knowledge that I knew of my presence, both inside myself and as a part of the totality surrounding me.

"So?" I asked as Louella sat in the chair facing me. "Did you and Hannah pick me to pieces? Did she encourage you to look at my better attributes or did she tell you to throw me out?"

"Mark, we didn't even talk about you. Not once. We talked about her, Hannah. Not you. And it's not good."

"What's not good?"

"She's is in a mess.... Mark, you've got to tell me the truth. You've always been a skeptical person. Did you figure out yet what to make of Victor's teachings? Do you still accept the whole thing?"

"You're asking me because Hannah is having trouble with him. Is that it?"

"Yes."

"Well, I suspect, Louella, that back when you gave up on Victor you weren't really rejecting his lessons. What you rejected was Victor. You disliked him and distrusted him. That's right, isn't it?"

"Yes. But we're talking about you. I'm asking what you believe."

"I see him as a flawed person. Of course I do. But so far, he hasn't told me anything that doesn't work for me. Maybe I'm living in two separate realities at once. I may not have sorted it out yet. But his ideas haven't stopped me from living in our so called real world. Not at all. Not so far, at least. So, what did Hannah tell you?"

"She says Victor's a liar and a manipulator. She called him an egomaniac. She says that what he's doing is creating an edifice devoted to his own self-glorification. In the beginning she felt exalted, thrilled to be living in a community where like minded people were attempting to create a better world... Those were her words. That's what she hoped would happen when she invited Victor onto the farm. Now she feels like a prisoner. Her own bedroom is the only place where she can breathe anymore."

"Has she tried to discuss this with Victor? With anyone other than you?" I asked.

"I don't think so, Mark. I'm afraid that we are the only people she trusts. And I certainly didn't have any idea of what to tell her. I just listened."

"Poor Hannah." I said. "You remember how this came about, don't you? She was going to quit The Quest. Maybe she had.... No. I remember. It was when Victor was caught fooling around with your friend Gertrude. His wife kicked him out of the house. That's when Hannah quit. Then her husband died and she was all alone on her farm. She was adrift without a rudder. Then Victor reappeared. He was going to save her. She gave over everything to be a part of his utopia. Together, they were going to give her a purpose in life."

"Yes, but that was two years ago. What about now? Can she

force everyone to pick up and leave? Can she simply say I want my farm back?"

"I don't know, Louella. She never told us exactly what kind of a deal they made. Did she sign any papers or do they just have an oral agreement? I'm sure somebody can tell her where she stands, legally. But I know I don't want to get squeezed between the two of them."

The week passed and nothing was different; as if I had never revealed my transgressions to Louella. I knew that she was deeply pained and I felt she wasn't about to reopen the wound. For now, at least, we would pretend nothing had happened. Also, it felt as though our six hundred mile separation was the anomaly and being together was how things were supposed to be.

Every night I spoke with Laura. Mostly I just listened as she spoke of her unhappiness and of her fears.

Louella never asked me what we had been talking about.

While I taught my class in the Lab School Louella spent much of her time with her old colleagues in the math department.

"They're treating me like a celebrity," she said after one of her visits. "They want to know everything I am working on and everything that I can tell them about computers."

Then, on Friday evening we were in our old Buick, driving to the airport; Louella to fly east, back to IBM, and I, west, to Dallas. The cool night was our first hint that the summer was over.

"Tell me again, Mark," Louella said, as she reached across the dashboard, raising the car's heat a few notches, "I can't believe that the college is paying your fare so that you can be a commuter and go hold that poor girl's hand whenever she's lonely."

"It isn't like that, and you know it, Louella. You said you believed me when I told you that whatever our relations were in the past, nothing is going to happen between Laura and me in the future. It's over, for both of us. You meant it, didn't you, when you said you believed me?"

"Yes, of course I did. I'm just saying I find it hard to believe that our esteemed college is paying you for baby sitting."

"It's much more than baby sitting and you know it. It's a month already since the killings on campus and the story is still all over the front pages. We're sitting on top of something very big and the college...well, Tom Lacy, has entrusted me with a huge responsibility."

We were already approaching the exit ramp for long term parking. Louella opened her pocketbook and rummaged around for her white gloves.

CHAPTER TWENTY-FIVE

ON SATURDAY I took Laura to the Tandy Craft store and bought her a tape recorder. The plan was that she should keep an oral diary as well as a written one. When we got back to her house she showed me an invitation from a student group at Berkeley. They were planning what they called a "teach in." This was one of the meetings being held on campuses across the country, educating students about how the Vietnam conflict came to be and how we got involved in it.

I called the organizer, telling him that Laura wasn't ready for public speaking but would like to send greetings to be announced at their meetings.

Also there was a message from a major broadcasting company. They wanted Laura to appear on the country's most watched morning broadcast.

"Never!" Laura said. I'm never going to use Zachary's death as an excuse to sell soap or toilet paper."

"Fine. Your job, for now, is to keep track of your feelings, and your thoughts. Let's see what happens. Don't get pushed into anything."

Together, we unpacked the tape recorder, plugged it in, and figured out how to use it.

Holding the microphone in front of Laura's face, I asked, "Are you sleeping any better, these days?"

"Hardly," she answered, pushing the instrument away.

"Then say that into the machine. Talk about how you are getting along with your family and with your oldest friends. All that stuff."

We set up a system for labeling and dating the reels of tape.

"Ok, let's try it again. Go ahead, hold the mike near your mouth and say something."

"What should I say?"

"You know what... Say shit—fuck. Say it a couple of times. Get so that you feel free to say whatever comes into your mind. If you can kill that censor whenever he or she shows up, then maybe you'll be surprised at what comes out. And you're the one who decides what to do with these tapes, what to use and what to get rid of. Say anything. Say everything."

"Will you get to hear what I record, Mark?"

"If you trust me as fully as I hope you will, yes. If you believe that I am here for you, completely, then yes, I'll listen. But it'll be your decision. I won't listen without your permission."

On Monday, returning home after school I found a message on my telephone answering machine. I was to return a call to one of the producers of *Worth Watching*, the Sunday night television news magazine.

I called the number.

"Thank you for calling back, Mr. Green. We understand that you are the person we should speak with so we can arrange an interview with Laura Steiner. We're planning to do a segment on the shooting of her child."

"No." I said. "I'm sorry, but Laura isn't granting any interviews until she's in better control of her emotions."

"But this isn't just any interview, this is *Worth Watching!* Millions of people will ...."

"No." I repeated. "Laura isn't ready yet. I'm really sorry."

"You don't understand, Mr. Green, This is the moment when the country is ready to see her. Not a month from now when it will be too late for her to communicate her say."

"Thanks for thinking about us." I said and ended the conversation by hanging up the phone. *Wow!* I thought. *Little David, standing up to Goliath. Big shot, Mark. You told them off, all right. It's like you're King Canute and you've just commanded the tides to roll back from the shore!*

Two days later I was in class, writing a homework assignment on the blackboard. Once the assignment was copied the class would be over for the day. Turning around, I saw Hannah Mays standing in the door, beckoning to me.

Hannah and I stepped out onto the school driveway. She was furious, hardly able to speak.

"I don't believe what's happening.....The farm has been invaded.... There are television crews all over the place, trucks, wires, people. Apparently Victor knew they were coming, but he never told me."

"Is it the crew from *Worth Watching*?"

"I think so. Victor is strutting around the place like a rooster. He's lecturing, right into the cameras, about The Quest, and he's talking about how Laura was one of his finest pupils."

"Bastards! Excuse me, Hannah. I can't believe they'd do that. Let's go see. Right now. I'll send my class home and follow you in my car."

When we got to the farm it seemed that most of the filming was completed. Lengths of garish, orange electrical cord were being wound up and returned to the trucks. Victor was still out-doors, standing with the reporter and the camera man. Seeing our cars arrive, my old Buick and Hannah's yellow pick-up truck, Victor must have identified us to the film crew because they left Victor and approached us even as we parked.

"Are you Mrs. Otto Mays, the owner of this farm?"

Hannah faced the bespectacled man who was dressed in suit and tie. She stood, arms crossed on her chest for a moment, then, feeling his presence uncomfortably close, she reached out and shoved him back.

"I am, and I never invited you onto my property."

The man caught his balance and with no hesitation turned to me.

"And you, Mr. Green, I understand that you are not only in con-tact with Laura Steiner, you have apparently appointed yourself as gatekeeper, deciding who she may talk with and who she mustn't talk to. Is that correct?"

I had a nasty and vulgar reply all prepared when I remembered that I represented not just Laura but Horace Mann College as well.

Instead, I took Hannah's arm and we walked away, unaware that they were filming our disappearing backsides.

"Mark, that man, Victor, and his whole entourage have got to get off of my property. I don't know how to make them move, but it has to happen."

"I'm so sorry you feel this way. I'm sorry it's come to this. I don't know what to tell you."

"But now, surely, you can see him for what he is, can't you? Are you going to help me or are you still on Victor's side?"

"I feel like you've backed me into a corner, Hannah."

"Hey! You there! Get your feet out of my strawberry patch!" Hannah barked at one of the film crew who was spooling up a cord.

"All right, Hannah. Let's get out of here. Let's go to the diner where we can talk."

We returned to our cars and drove to the diner.

We sat in a booth. I ordered a coke and Hannah ordered tea.

Even before our drinks arrived Hanna started to unburden herself. "I need to tell you how this all came about," she said. "There never was any written contract or lease involving The Quest. Victor suggested bringing his operation to the farm and I told him 'yes'. That's all there was to it."

"But you agreed. You invited him, and now you've changed your mind. Why?"

"Mark, that was a terrible time for me. Otto had just died. I was all alone and my head wasn't clear. It seemed like the right thing to do. Now I see how wrong I was."

"Well, I said,"I don't know the first thing about what the law will say. But I've got some idea of who might tell you. Do you know Bernie Madison? His kid used to be in my class. He's one of the college's lawyers and I think he does some real estate too. Do you want me to set up a meeting with him?"

"Please."

We parted with a warm hug.

Worth Watching announced its entire broadcast, next Sunday, would be devoted to the war protestors; particularly the ever widening campus demonstrations.

Sunday I went to the farm in time for dinner, before the scheduled broadcast.

As the others were settling themselves at the table I took Hannah aside and whispered to her, "I talked to Bernie this afternoon." "He's going to be away for a couple of weeks, but next month we can set up a meeting. The three of us can get together at his office and he won't charge us anything. We'll just talk, informally."

"Thanks, Mark. That will make me very happy."

Her face showed anything but happiness.

After supper we all gathered in the living room in front of the television set, tuned to the program *Worth Watching*. All, that is, except for Hannah who chose not to watch, but retired directly to her bedroom.

The first of the twelve minute segments was devoted to Laura Steiner. There were still-photos of her progress through grade school, high school and college. Somehow, they got a copy of the photograph showing Zachary smiling up at the camera from astride his tricycle. There were interviews with Laura's Dallas neighbors and footage of her going from the car to her house. They showed what little footage of the actual riot existed and then they focused on "the commune, just off campus" where they said Laura had been living with her son, Zachary.

We all moved closer to the screen when the scene shifted to the farm and the interview with Victor.

Victor conducted himself with aplomb. He refused to commit himself as to the justice or injustice of the conflict. Rather, he made it clear that Laura's fateful presence at the demonstration had nothing to do with her quest for self awareness which everyone at the farm was a part of. Victor wouldn't allow himself to condemn whoever it was who fired the bullets at the students. Rather, Victor described those actions as "blind obedience to false ideas; an example of what he called 'sleepwalking'.

The cameras then shifted to Hannah and me, arriving, refusing to speak, and walking away.

The segment concluded with the producer, piously intoning, "This tragedy, a twenty-one year old mother having her infant shot to death in her very arms, may be the grimmest tragedy to come out of this war so far. In any case, it is certain to be the one of the first images called to mind whenever one thinks about these difficult times."

I left before the film credits were over, got into my car and drove out the lane. Entering the county road I automatically reached out to turn on the radio. Country and western music filled the car. A minute later I remembered Victor's injunction: "Do just one thing at a time. When you are driving you should be driving with all your attention, and when you are listening to music you should listen to that music with all your attention." I switched off the radio and the car was filled with a palpable silence.

I was angry, angry at Victor and angry at myself. I was confused. I was conflicted. My thoughts emerged in a jumble.

How exciting to have seen myself on national television! Stop it Mark, this isn't about you. It's about Laura. But it's about Hannah and Victor too. Poor Hannah. She's in a mess. She's asked me to help her, and there isn't anyone but me who can help her. Has it got to the point where I have to choose between Hannah and Victor? Sure, I like being part of The Quest. I like Victor's ideas, even if I don't trust him. Sure, he is using Gurdjief's teachings for his own aggrandizement.... But didn't Gurdjief treat his own disciples the very same way? On the other hand, who'm I kidding? It's a great intellectual exercise, and it is the biggest part of my social life. But is it real? I don't live it...I rarely 'wake up' to my presence. Mostly, I live as if I've never heard a single one of these words that I find so easy to parrot back to my 'beginner's class' at the farm. Am I faking it, waiting to see if any of it is true or not? And meanwhile, what about Hannah? I doubt there's much that anyone can do for her. She made a deal and she's stuck with it.

But all that's the easy stuff. Look where I've got to...unbelievable. For God's sake, my retreating backside has just been viewed by millions of

people. Okay, so the fact that America saw my backside is no big deal com-
pared to Laura's loss of her chid... but now I've become part of something
really big. I'm just beginning to understand where I fit in. What about my
new role in the college? Am I going to pull it off, or screw it up? I expect I
can handle it, but I sure wish Louella were here to reason with me.

Then, without conscious thought, the radio was turned on again
and country and western music, once more, filled the car.

I parked under my carport and entered the house. The bulb
on the answering machine was blinking. It was Louella saying, "I
watched you on television. You were marvelous. Call me."

I dialed immediately. Louella wanted to share her excitement at
seeing me on national television but I was more anxious to discuss
my frustrations, not my so-called achievements.

"Louella, listen, I'm still furious that he allowed *Worth Watching*
onto the property. I told them Laura wasn't ready to be seen in public. Did that slow them down? Not for a second!"

"Calm yourself. We know what reporters are like," Louella said,
"but more important, did Victor know you didn't want them to do
the program?"

"He must have known...But it wouldn't have mattered. He wasn't
going to turn away his moment of fame.... his moment in the spot-
light. He wasn't thinking of Laura for a second. It was all about
Victor!"

"So, you've finally come around to being angry with Victor, have
you?"

"Angry, yes, but I'm not ready to choose sides. I guess I'm willing
to help Hannah. Victor had his followers even before he had Hannah
and the farm. It wont be the end of The Quest if he has to take them
somewhere else."

"But what about you, Mark? You'll have to take a side now. You
can't have it both ways, can you?"

"I don't want to talk any more tonight, Louella. I don't even
want to think about it. I want to go to bed and sleep, and wake up

tomorrow and go teach my students. Enough bickering. Good night sweetheart."

I hung up before my wife could answer.

Then I thought some more. *Does this mean that I am through with The Quest? No more lessons to teach? No more classes with Victor? ... That's not what I want—to chuck it all... What I want is for Hannah to get her farm back. But I'm going to stick with The Quest as long as I can... I'm not rejecting it. Yes,... Victor, you'll have to be the one. You'll have to throw me out... Let's see how vindictive he turns out be!*

CHAPTER TWENTY-SIX

BY THE end of September I'd been to Dallas two more times and was thrilled to know Laura was assiduously keeping to her task as diarist, even while she began to assume a new role as poster child and reluctant spokesperson for the peace movement.

Then, the first weekend in October, I accompanied her, all the way to California, where she spoke to a rally on the Berkeley campus.

Louella had once referred to my role as "glorified baby-sitter," but it wasn't that. Laura was still terrified at facing an audience. She needed me there, at her side, assuring her.

I was still wrestling with my own decision: whether or not to break with Victor, when Bernie Madison returned to campus and phoned me, stating his readiness to meet with us.

Early afternoon, after dismissing my class, I met Hannah outside Bernie's home, a simple frame house on a tree-lined street. We climbed the porch steps and let ourselves through the door marked "office." Bernie rose from behind his raised desk, greeted us, shook our hands, and indicated that we should sit in the two straight-backed, leather- cushioned chairs facing his desk.

Bernie was of medium height with curly brown hair beginning to turn gray. He'd first come to Horace Mann as a student and then upon finishing law school in New York he'd come right back to open a practice in Cold Springs. But all those years in Ohio had done nothing to soften his New York accent or mannerisms.

"Oh, don't pay any attention to that," he said when he saw me staring at the framed poster behind his desk. It was a photograph of Abraham Lincoln and across Lincoln's torso were his words "A lawyer's stock in trade is his time and his advice. It is only just that he charge for them."

"No charge for today's meeting. Just tell me what's bothering you."

I described Hannah's situation as fully as I could. There was no need to identify Hannah's farm as the place where Laura Steiner had been living. Everyone in town knew that by now: and almost everyone in the rest of the country too.

"Can you add anything to Mark's story?" Bernie asked Hannah.

"Only that it has become unbearable, living with those people. And the farm is all that I've got."

"Well," Bernie said, leaning back in his chair, entwining the fingers of his hands and spreading them across his belly, "my gut reaction, Hannah, is that you have a pretty good case to kick them out. They haven't been there long enough to establish squatters' rights. True, they spent money on the property, and they put in sweat equity too. But that doesn't guarantee them rights to the property. They might just sue you for the money they've put into the property, but if they've been living there for free then they have received something for their efforts."

"Another problem, you may encounter," Bernie continued, still speaking directly to Hannah, "is, what about the apartments they have built? Are they up to code? Did they secure proper building permits? And what about the school? Is it licensed? Is the barn properly fire proofed?"

"I have no idea about any of that. I'm not sure if the work was up to code or not. The members, I guess I should say 'we.' We did most of the work ourselves."

"Then," said Bernie, "there's one other problem. Even if the court finds in your favor, you may still have a hard time kicking them out because tenants, even those living for free, have lots of rights in this state and if they take you to housing court it may be a long, expensive procedure."

"But are you willing to take Hannah's case, Bernie?" I asked.

"And by taking it, are you signaling that you think we have a good chance of winning?"

"There's always a chance," he replied. "You two should take some time to think about whether or not you want to hire me to take you on. I'll be charging you forty dollars an hour, which I assure you is a fair rate. I have no idea how long it will take and I have no idea if we will win."

Hannah spoke up. "There is no mortgage on the farm. Otto was so proud when we finished paying it. I'm willing to go back to the bank if I must. We'll use the farm as, what do you call it? Collateral? Do it, Mr Madison."

"Oh," Bernie seemed to recollect something. "Of course you've already asked Victor to vacate and he's refused? Is that correct Hannah?"

Hannah hesitated, cleared her throat, swallowed, and then answered, "No. I never told Victor that he has to get out. Nothing. Not yet. I've been afraid to."

"Well, that comes first. Talk to the man and see what his position is. Maybe you won't need me at all.

As we were leaving Bernie took me by the arm and said, "Congratulations, Mark, I understand they've made you the custodian of one big chunk of history!"

"Yeh, sort of. Thanks."

"It's important for the college, Mark. You should be proud."

The lab school closes at noon, for a full hour. Most everyone goes home for lunch. Often, I'd been been taking my lunches in the college cafeteria, but recently I'd begun going to the faculty restaurant, a frame bungalow on the far side of the campus, but near my Lab School.

It was a chilly October day when I found Al Kramer there, seated by himself. I joined him.

"Nice of you to sit with me, Mark."

"What does that mean?"

"Well, it seems to me that you've been keeping yourself kind of aloof, one might say."

"Out with it, Al. No hiding behind that beard of yours. What's bothering you?"

"You rarely come to eat at the farm anymore and when you do show up you and Hannah go off to some corner where you can conspire, or so it seems. Rumor has it that you and Hannah are in cahoots, trying to get rid of Victor and the rest of us. I've even heard that you want to take over The Quest. Is that your plan?"

"Al, wake up and pay some attention. It's Hannah's farm, you know."

"So I'm right!"

"No you're not. Not as far as The Quest is concerned, you aren't..."

That was as far as we got when two professors from the math department, friends of Louella's whom I hardly knew, came in and asked if they could join us.

"Please. Have a seat." I said.

They sat. I couldn't remember their names, but by introducing them to Al, I got them to remind me of who they were.

The younger of the two was full of enthusiasm. He turned right to me and said, "Your protege, Laura Steiner, is doing some wonderful things these days!"

"She's hardly my protege." I replied. "She's created this role of 'student leader' and 'anti-war spokesman' all by herself."

Now the older of the two spoke, a grey haired, tenured professor who, I remembered, had long ago terrified Louella.

"But we know it's more than that, Mark. When Laura Steiner spoke at the rally, at Berkeley, we all watched on television. You had to be at her side, to introduce her, and you practically held her up, she was so nervous."

"I suppose you're right," I said. "Actually, it's amazing what's happened in such a short time. She's really begun to flourish. She still gets nervous, but she overcomes it."

The math professors did their best to elicit more particulars which they would then be able to pass on to others as their very own contact with celebrity.

I told them as little as courtesy would allow. I did say that I rarely saw Laura anymore because she no longer needed my support, but that she was keeping extensive written records of everything happening to her and soon we would be shaping those records into a senior thesis. I didn't tell them about the publishers who were already lining up with offers of book contracts. I finished my lunch, stood up, and said, "I have to be back at school in six minutes. It's good to have spoken to the two of you."

"Send my regards to your wife," said the older one.

I turned to Al and said, "We need to continue this discussion. We've barely started and I don't think you understand me at all."

Al and I never got to complete our discussion.

Another week went by and Hannah still hadn't gathered the strength she would need to face Victor, to demand that he, and all of his followers, vacate her farm.

CHAPTER TWENTY-SEVEN

NOVEMBER. Hannah still hadn't found the opportunity, or perhaps the will, to confront Victor. To my own embarrassment, I too had said nothing.

Again, I flew to Dallas to confer with Laura about how she might organize her rapidly growing pile of folders, audio tapes and newspaper clippings. Just one day before I arrived, Newsweek Magazine had appeared with Laura's picture on its cover: a photograph of her addressing a teach-in at Brown University, the caption read, "A new leader emerges, energizing the student protests."

The Laura who met me at the exit ramp was a very different person from the defeated and deflated soul who had met me in the same place only three months earlier. Laura smiled to see me and we embraced. I thrilled to feel the rush of energy emanating from her. Never had she seemed so vigorous.

As we drove to her parents' home, she spoke non-stop. I said very little.

"I've been doing just as you told me to," she said. "I'm writing everything down. But I've got to tell you how exciting it's been."

She bubbled with tales of the fascinating people she'd been meeting in the peace movement. During her soliloquy, unable to squeeze in a word, I did have time to notice that she wasn't as skinny as I remembered. Her ever-present dungarees were replaced by a neat black skirt which rode high above her knees as she shifted the gears of her father's new sports car. I felt a pleasant stirring in my crotch and let my left hand gently brush the side of her thigh.

Without a pause in her monologue, Laura took my hand firmly in hers and sent it back somewhere near the swelling in my pants.

At the house, Laura's parents greeted us and then disappeared, leaving us in the study where stacks of papers were piled on the couch, awaiting us.

I cleared enough space so we might sit together but Laura, quite deliberately, dragged a chair close to the couch and sat opposite me.

The hormones that drove me were in control, stronger than what little restraint remained. The promises I'd made to myself and to Louella were not forgotten, but powerless. I stood up, walked behind Laura and put my arms around her shoulders.

"Mark! Stop it!"

Laura shook herself free.

"We're here to work. If you've come here for sex, you've come too late. That's over. You're here because we have a job to do and don't forget it. Not for a moment."

I wasn't embarrassed; I knew Laura too well to feel embarrassed. And I didn't feel crushed by rejection. It was just the opposite.

Clearly, Laura wasn't going to respond to my advances, and I was pleased to realize that I felt relief. It pleased me to know we would work together without the complications that would follow if we were to become lovers again. It pleased me even more to know that when I get home on Sunday and phone my wife in Peekskill that I won't be picking my words carefully, hiding my guilt and fearing discovery.

"Okay. I'll do my best to remember... You know what, Laura? You're right. Thank you for reminding me."

Next morning, soon after we began working our way through the piled up papers, the telephone rang. Laura rose from the couch to answer.

"Hello?"

As she stood there I watched her face change. Her alert expression dissolved. Her face went pale. Her eyes widened in terror. Without speaking, she returned the receiver to its cradle and sat beside me on the couch.

"Hold me," she said.

She was no longer the confident person who had rejected my advances. This was the terrified Laura of recent memory.

"What is it?" I asked as I cradled her in my arms.

"They want to kill me. He called me 'a mother fucking commie cunt.' He said 'I'm watching you, and as soon as your Yankee lover goes home I'm gonna shoot you.'"

I held Laura tight. I too experienced the chill of defenseless vulnerability.

"Is this the first time he's called on your phone?"

"No. Sometimes he calls and doesn't say anything. I just hear him breathing. Sometimes he says nasty things about Zachary. But this is the first time he's said he's going to kill me."

"Do you have any idea who he is?"

"No."

"Have you told the police?"

"Mark. This is Texas, remember? We're only a few miles from where they shot Kennedy. I'm not going to them for help."

As she spoke of the police I felt some resolve returning to Laura's limp body. I held her in silence for a while longer. My eyes focused on her father's gun rack opposite us.

"Laura, you once told me you used to go hunting with your father and that you're a good shot, Remember? Do you think you might load one of those pistols and keep it with you?"

"I could do that."

"Do it! Do you know where he keeps the key to the cabinet?"

"Sure."

"We're not going to accomplish any more this morning." I said. "Let's go somewhere. We'll have strong coffee and then we'll go for a walk. But, this time, when you go out on the street, you'll be an armed Texan."

On Sunday we were better able to concentrate on our work and accomplished a lot. We started a scrapbook of clippings about her campus speeches.

"You know," I said, "these speeches keep getting better and

better. It's almost like there's a direct correlation between how good your speeches are and how many more troops President Johnson sends over there. Each good speech seems to elicit another five thousand or so."

"No sarcasm, Mister Professor," she said, elbowing me in the ribs.

Essentially, our task was a form of triage. Some of the material was to be shaped into a senior thesis, but the notion of what shape her thesis should take was still vague. We agreed that it would be much more than a diary. Essentially, I believed, it should chronicle Laura's own understanding of why Johnson was fighting a war in Viet Nam, how we got there and how we might get out.

And there was her book to write—likely, more than one. We hadn't yet chosen among the book offers; there was a stack of tempting requests and no rush to pick. We still hadn't sorted out the difference between what belonged in a thesis and what belonged in a publishable manuscript, so we kept our options open, sorting her material by category.

That evening I was to take the red-eye, back to Ohio. There still remained quite a lot to be sorted, so I offered to take home a pile which I could go through on the airplane. Loaded down with diaries and with scraps of jotted down random thoughts, I parted from Laura.

"I could tell you 'don't be afraid' but that would be silly. Be vigilant and let's hope that he's just a harmless kook."

"In any case," she said, "when I go out now, I won't be a helpless target any more. He'd better watch himself when he's watching me!"

I kissed her 'goodbye' and traveled east.

The red-eye, as I'd expected, was uncrowded. I deposited my papers on the empty seats next to me and began sorting out the random notes and old letters that Laura had given me. Reading her father's letters, I was impressed with his devotion to her. Then I found one from her mother, written a year and a half ago:

"Laura, so you've found yourself a fellow!!! Good. A teacher! I'm pleased. No, dear, it doesn't upset me that he's a married man. But just because he's married, and on top of that, a college graduate doesn't mean he won't make you pregnant and then up and disappear, like the no-account who got you that way in high school. Take care!!!

Love and hugs.

Your mother."

Weird letter! Hardly sounds like something a mother would write. But that explains, I guess, why her parents are always leaving the two of us alone. And why her parents have always been so accepting of me. There aren't many secrets in this world, are there?

I placed Laura's diary notes in a separate manila envelope. Among these notes were a few personal letters which I separated and returned to the 'letters' folder.

One of these seized my attention. The handwriting was familiar: a graceful handwriting—carefully well-formed letters. There was no mistaking Victor's distinctive style. It was dated July 8th, 1964. I noted the date, just a month before Laura's world fell apart. I remembered that she had gone home to Texas for a brief visit.

I read the letter;

"My dear Laura,

I'm missing you terribly but I know it's only for a week and then you'll be back. Little Victor cries most of the night. I lie there, unable to sleep through the noise. I grind my teeth and put the pillow over my head. It doesn't help. And the only way I can fall asleep is if I concentrate. I visualize the two of us lying together, me rubbing up against your body. We're belly to belly...slowly I bunch up your nightgown... lift it over your oh so thin arms... I take one of your breasts between my lips. I'm sucking, biting, sucking, biting.... then the other breast. Oh Laura, soon you will be back and we can begin where we left off. Until then.... I'll lie here, remembering every moment we've spent together and I await your return, my sweetness. It will be so glorious...again and again and again...I can't stop myself...Ohhhhh.

Affectionately yours,

Victor Lamotta"

I put the letter aside and closed my eyes. At once, I became aware of the roar of the jet engine outside my window.

Hah! You forgot, didn't you? You're on an airplane, going back to Cold Springs, Ohio. So what am I supposed to feel? Jealousy? Indignation? Anger? I realized that the letter had left me with a particularly hard erection.

Did she want me to know? Did she care?

I decided that she must have wanted me to know. *What a bastard, that man!..... Am I any better?* Then my mind flashed back to the evening before my first visit to Dallas. I was so pleased with myself. The college had just made me Laura's mentor. Somehow, Victor knew I was going. He phoned me and, in his most authoritative voice, he commanded, "Don't go there, Mark. I've had a premonition. Something terrible will happen if you go there."

Of course, I ignored his warning. But I was mystified. What was motivating him? At the time I thought he was trying to establish his dominance over me. Now I was sure it was jealousy. He wanted Laura for himself. And then I thought of the weekly consultations which Victor regularly holds with each of his students. "Is that what goes on during those meetings?"

Now my mind was racing. I recalled the limited hints Victor had given our group about Gurdjief's ideas on sex. "The body has three main centers—intellectual, emotional and physical," he said. "But there is also a sexual center operating within each of those three centers. I'll tell you about it when you are ready to hear it. But you aren't ready yet."

Did Victor believe that he was operating on a level beyond what the rest of us could understand? Is that what he meant when he defended abandoning his wife and taking up with Gertrude? What he said was, "I'm doing it for the good of The Quest."

The sudden thump of tires striking the runway, and the airplane's swaying from side to side jerked me back to attention. I realized how I had been savoring my anger, how rewarding to have been given evidence; proof of Victor's character faults.

CHAPTER TWENTY-EIGHT

MONDAY AFTERNOON, my first day back from Texas, I dismissed my class at three and drove straight to the farm. The time had come to confront Victor.

Along the way I thought out what I might say to him. There were so many choices and I rehearsed each of them.

It wasn't until approaching the turn onto the farm-lane that I recalled Victor's own injunction; "It's futile," he often said, "to rehearse a conversation. Instead of planning what you're going to say next, you should listen, observe, pay attention—then, when it's your turn to speak you'll know what to say and the words will come."

Good advice! But still, I found myself rehearsing. Then it occurred to me; *Maybe Hannah's already confronted him, while I was away in Texas. That'll certainly make it easier for me. I'll go up and see her first.*

I parked and entered the house.

Silence. With the outside light quickly fading, the living room was practically dark. Looking into the dining room I saw the corner shrine; a statue of the seated Buddha, a single candle flickering.

I went upstairs and knocked on Hannah's door and waited to be invited in. When she opened I saw that the curtains were drawn and the light from a single table lamp scarcely dispelled the gloom. Hannah was dressed in a cotton nightgown and a flannel robe.

"Oh, it's you." she said. "I didn't hurry to answer because I thought it would be Patricia again. She keeps pushing me to come downstairs, whether I feel like it or not. Sit down, Mark. You're back from Dallas again, aren't you? What have you got to tell me?"

I closed the door behind us, hugged Hannah, and still standing, asked, "Did you talk to him? Did you tell him you want him off your property?"

Hannah visibly slumped, turned, and eased herself into the armchair. I sat facing her.

"No. Maybe Bernie Madison should tell him," she said. "Wouldn't it be stronger, coming from a lawyer?"

"I don't think so... Maybe... No. Don't you remember? Bernie said you have to take the first step, Hannah. Do you want me to do it with you?"

"Yes."

"Right now?'

"No. I'm not up to it. Not now."

"How about I come over tomorrow, right after school?"

"Thank you, Mark. That will be better."

I left, and returned the following afternoon. We found Victor in the kitchen and asked him to come out with us to the porch.

When we were all seated, Victor started the conversation with a challenge.

"I sense there's some sort of conspiracy afoot," he said. "Are the two of you really conspiring or am I mistaken?"

"You talk, Hannah," I said.

She spoke, without hesitation: "Victor, it's taken me a long time, but now I know I made a terrible mistake when I let you talk yourself and your group onto my property. It was my mistake and now I want to end it. I want you, and The Quest to be gone from here."

"Just like that? Immediately?"

Hannah was no longer slouching in her chair. She sat erect and spoke decisively.

"Yes, as soon as possible. Immediately might not be possible, but it would be fine."

Victor thought for a moment. His expression didn't vary. There was no bodily movement from which we might guess how Hannah's ultimatum was affecting him. Then, looking directly at Hannah, Victor replied, "You know, Hannah, you being a part of The Quest has been very good for you. You are a much stronger person now than you were two years ago. Yes, I know you are feeling conflict and irritation. This experience is good for you. This is how you will continue to grow—by rubbing up against what is hardest for you, by seeing what is happening in your head, by consciously examining your feelings, by overcoming your negativity."

"No, Victor!" Hannah exploded. "I don't want you telling me I'm wrong. I want you out of my life!"

"But Hannah, think clearly. We've created homes here for people who need us. We've built a school. You can't undo all of this on a whim."

Now I joined in.

"Not on a whim, Victor. Hannah knows what she wants. We don't know what her rights are. Not yet. But we've gone to a lawyer who will tell us how to remove you from this farm."

"I understand you, Mark," Victor said. "I know you, maybe better than you know yourself. But it appears you have chosen to leave The Quest, so this is between Hannah and her people here—not you. I don't believe it is in Hannah's best interests for you to be telling her what to think."

Hannah stood.

"No Victor! Don't you dare blame Mark for my decisions."

She turned to me, spread her arms, palms uplifted, shrugging her shoulders. "That's how it is now, Mark. I'll go on being a prisoner in my own home until Bernie Madison finds a way to make Victor leave. But at least, now, Victor knows what I want. Thank you, Mark, for being here for me."

Hannah spoke to me as though Victor no longer existed. Then she turned away, walked into the house, and up to her room. Saying nothing, I left Victor on the porch and drove home.

CHAPTER TWENTY-NINE

CHRISTMAS WAS approaching. Bernie was working on Hannah's case but doubted he'd have anything to tell us until after the holidays.

Instead of Louella coming west to Cold Springs, I went east and spent my vacation with her in New York.

Much of the drive from the airport up to Peekskill in a rental car was occupied with my thoughts about what to share with Louella.

Can I tell her what I've just learned about Victor's dalliance with Laura? For God's sake, who'd believe it? I hardly believe it. The same time that Laura and I were up there doing it in the hayloft, Laura was making it with Victor as well. OK, there's no need to convince Louella that Victor is scum. She's already decided that on her own. Come to think about it, I'm no better a man than he is. What's different? Were we both using Laura, or was she using both of us? Anyway, Louella knows about my affair with Laura—because I told her. It hurt her terribly when I confessed. Face it, I told her for my own sake, not for Louella's good. Well, we've put that behind us, more or less. But dare I open it up again? No. It's better not to talk about it.

Then the magnificent sweep of the Hudson River appeared in front of me. Soon I was at my wife's red brick apartment complex, climbing to the second floor and ringing the bell.

Louella greeted me with a warm embrace. Holding my two hands, she stepped back and said, "I've got some good news to tell you."

"Wait. Kiss me again." She did. Then we entered, I pulled her to the couch, again wrapped my arms around her and said, "OK, now tell me the good news."

"Daddy has had his term cut short. Not a pardon, he's been

commutated or something. He's getting out of Sing Sing on the first of the Year."

"Stupendous! How come?"

"He isn't sure how it came about. Somebody, one of his buddies must have remembered him and pushed for it."

"Your mother must be thrilled—you too."

"Well, at least I'm happy. My mother is less so.

She's not sure that she wants Dad back in the house. She says she's got used to being without him. Mostly, I think, she's ashamed of what he did and she can't face going anywhere with him and being thought of as 'that embezzler's wife.'"

"Have you talked to him about what he's going to do?"

"Well, The Board of Education won't have anything to do with him. That's for sure. But he's hoping to find something with one of the suppliers he used to buy from. He thinks his connections have to be worth something."

"No. I mean what about him and your mother."

"I don't know. We'll see."

During the ten days I spent with Louella the issue between her mother and father remained unsettled. It seemed the whole family was unsettled. Only a month earlier Louella's sister gave up on her own marriage, left her husband, and taking her six-year-old daughter, went to live with her mother.

Louella was involved with her family's problems, but I didn't sense that she was terribly upset or stressed. What I gathered, mostly, during our ten days of reunion was how much she still enjoyed her work as a scientist, or mathematician, or whatever it was she was doing for I.B.M. that was beyond my comprehension.

A couple of days before New Years I returned to Horace Mann College, preparing to face my lab-school students and a new class of college students in The Education Department.

*

My first morning home Patricia called me from the farm.

"Hello, Mark. May I come over to talk?"

"Is Victor sending you?"

"Not really. No, not really. I just need to talk with you."

"Sure. Okay. You can come right now if you want to. Sooner is better than later," I said, "because they're predicting snow this afternoon."

Patricia arrived half an hour later. She entered, wearing a gray overcoat and a woolen scarf that covered her hair and ears.

"This is the hardest time of the year for me." She said. "My blood hasn't thickened yet and I've been shivering since Christmas."

"Well, take off your coat and welcome. You've never been here before, have you?"

"No, you've never invited me."

"I am guilty there and I apologize. How's your husband these days? I'm surprised that he isn't the one Victor would send to talk with me."

"Jeremy is fine," she answered. "He isn't here. He's in Texas again, at the commune. He's getting more instruction in the esoteric movements and dances. He's really become good at it. He brings it all back to us, but it's slow, hard stuff, learning those movements. Did you know that Jeremy quit his job with the law firm? He's teaching with me now in our little school. And that's really what I came to talk about."

Patty now leaned forward in her chair and looked intently into my eyes. She took a deep breath and began speaking. Her words carried just a hint of having been carefully rehearsed.

"Mark, everyone tells me what a good job you are doing at the Lab School. Well, our school in the barn is off to a good start too. We opened in September with eleven kids. When we start back next Monday we expect to have eighteen. Rita just got custody of her sons, so they're going to live with her and Al in the Winnebago, and attend to our school. The others all come from families that want something special for their kids."

"I guess what I'm saying is that there's room in this town for real choices in education. There's your lab school. There's the public school. And there's our school, where children learn by waking up to the real world."

"Okay," I interrupted. "I'm happy that you are doing well, but why are you telling me this?"

"Because your colleague, your lawyer, Bernie Madison just served us, each of us at the farm, with eviction papers. According to these papers we are illegally trespassing on Hannah Mays' property and we are to evacuate the premises immediately."

"And what do you expect me to say, Patty?"

"Don't pretend that you aren't the one who is doing this to us. We know that you are behind every decision that Hannah makes."

Patty's accusation upset me. I was sure that it was unfair: equally sure that I'd never convince Patty of its unfairness. Instead, I stood up and went to the window.

"Look Patty. It's started snowing! Tiny little flakes. I've heard that when it starts out like this it'll be a big one."

"Mark, sit down and pay attention to what I'm saying."

I sat down and Patricia continued, "I spoke to Jeremy on the phone last night. I called him in Texas. He's sure that we are within our rights to continue with things just as they are. You know, and we all know that Victor and Hannah never bothered to draw up any papers. It was a verbal agreement. Hannah invited us onto the farm and we've been taking care of her and taking care of the farm ever since. She can't just change her mind and tell us 'be gone.' Jeremy assured us that a verbal agreement is still binding, a contract. He says that the only problem with a verbal agreement is that it's hard to prove that it happened. But for the past two years we've been living on the farm and making improvements. What more proof could you ask for?"

"Patty, if it comes down to a legal battle is Jeremy going to represent you?"

"I suppose he would. But it isn't going to come to that, Mark, you've got to talk to her. Make her understand that she can't play with our lives like this. Reason with her. She'll listen to you."

Enough, I thought. *There's no way I'm going to make Patty see things my way, or Hannah's way for that matter. Nor is she going to change my mind.*

Stymied, I stood up, stepped to the window, crossed my arms and looked out at the falling snow.

"Answer me, Mark!"

I turned around and faced her.

"Patricia, I do have immense respect for what you and Jeremy are accomplishing at your school. But that isn't the issue. More important, right now, I think you'd better go home before the roads get too slippery to drive on."

Patricia stood, let out a "humph" of disgust, hurriedly put on her coat, and at the door, said, "I'd hoped for more understanding, Mark."

I didn't answer. Instead, I again turned and looked out the window. I heard the slamming door and watched her feet leaving impressions in the rapidly accumulating snow. Then I went back to my desk where unfinished lesson plans for the coming week, were strewn: plans for my fifth and sixth graders and for the college freshmen whom I would soon be facing for the first time.

Patricia's visit left me unable to concentrate on my work. My thoughts swirled around The Quest, around Victor, and around what a huge part of my life this had been for the past several years, and about how big a part it still is:

There is so much about The Quest that I respect. I like Patty, if not her pompous husband. She's right, her school is a good thing. She's teaching what she learned from Victor and it all seems to be valid... no, more than valid... worthwhile. Victor always says "don't take any of this on faith. Try it and see if it works." ... For me it seems to work. So why am I aiding Hannah? ... It's because Victor is an opportunist, a conniver, a dishonest person ... and Hannah, whom Victor's making miserable, she's my friend. But what about Patricia and all of the others who follow Victor?

They're friends too, or at least they used to be. ... He's using them. That's what's happening. He's using them to build an image for himself. And in the process he's making Hannah miserable... "

I realized I was day-dreaming: building an imaginary conversation in my own head. *Wake up Mark! You're here, at your desk. Go back to work!*

CHAPTER THIRTY

IT WAS late when I got home from the first of my once-a-week meetings of my *Foundations of Education* class but I was too high not to telephone, to share my excitement with my wife.

I dialed and she answered sleepily.

"Hello?" she mumbled.

"Sweetheart. Wake up. I need to tell you how it went."

"What went? What are you talking about in the middle of the night?"

"It's not the middle of the night....not yet. Louella, I just got home from teaching my first college class. I loved it! And better still, I think that they loved it."

No longer sleepy, nor confused, Louella said, "Oh, that's wonderful. I'm so glad you called. Tell me everything."

"Well, to start, because it's an evening class, half my students are commuters. They live off campus. They work in the daytime and they're motivated learners. They set the tone for the kids just out of high school. "

"Okay, go on."

"When I introduced myself, and told them that my day job is teaching in the Lab School, that really excited them. One said to me,'That means you actually know how to teach, doesn't it?'"

But here's the best part.... I've learned so much from Victor... Remember, he told us about the three centers in the body? The moving center, the emotional center and the intellectual center."

"I remember. But we're through with him, aren't we? Don't keep quoting Victor to me."

"No. Listen! Victor told us once that a lesson is most effective if it can reach all three centers at the same time. So that's what I did. I gave them copies of John Dewey's pamphlet 'My Pedagogical Credo' to read. I told them it would be hard to understand, but they should get into groups of either three or four people and go over it, paragraph by paragraph, explaining to each other what Dewey is saying. That took more than half our time.

Then each group appointed a reporter whose job was to give us a summary of what John Dewey was saying. Next, I told them, "Everyone pick a partner, but not someone you've been working with before. You and your partner should discuss what points you might want to cover in writing your own personal pedagogical credo. Each of you, make a list of what might go into it."

Finally, I told them their homework assignment. They have to go ahead and write their own educational credo. I said it'll be interesting to see if your beliefs change in any way during this course or over the next four years.'"

"That's good, Mark. I like what you did. But you don't have to keep saying that you are using Victor's ideas. It isn't personal, private wisdom. He didn't invent any of it. He learned bits and pieces of ancient wisdom and you learned it from him. Now it's yours. Enough of giving all the credit to Victor."

"Thanks. I'll try to remember that."

"Can I go back to sleep now?"

"Sure you can. Thanks for listening. I love you. Sleep well."

I hung up the phone, went into the bedroom and got into my pajamas. Returning to the living room I punched the button on my answering machine that had been blinking all the while. There were two messages.

The first was from Bernie Madison:

"Well, Mark... this is Bernie.... It looks as if we're gonna have a fight on our hands. They have a lawyer, some fellow named Jeremy O'Hara. He's local but I've never heard of him. Anyway, he says that they have no intention of vacating the premises and that if we bring them to court they will counter sue for breach of contract. I guess we three should meet and decide what's next. Give me a call."

*

The second message was from Laura.

"Hi Ho buster! I'm at the Dallas airport on my way to Michigan, like we said, to talk at the conference, but most important, I'm getting together with the leadership of SDS. That's 'Students for a Democratic Society' in case you didn't know. They want to coordinate my speeches from here on. So if it works, you won't have to do it any more. Talk to you tomorrow. Ta ta."

Of course the message hurt me. It stung!

So she's through with me. It was short and sweet, my brush with fame—and now she doesn't need me anymore, I thought as I went off to bed. No sooner did I lie down than the telephone rang. I got up and went back into the living room. It was Laura again.

"Hello Mark. Did you get my message?"

"Yes. Where are you?"

"I'm still at the airport. My flight is delayed and I want to fill you in on what's happening. The college is still paying my phone bills, right?"

"Yeh. Sure. What's up?"

We talked for half an hour, until her flight was announced. She didn't have anything important to say, rather, I could tell that she wanted the reassurance of knowing I was still there for her. I was her sounding board, her connection to reality.

When Laura went off to her flight and I returned to bed I was content, pleased that Laura still valued my participation in her life. I was happy she'd found friends, people with whom she shared a mission, but even happier to be reassured that she still relied on me to keep her on track. She wasn't through with me after all.

On a bright, frigid, afternoon Hannah and I were in The Lemon Peel, a student hangout which mimicked the idea of a New York, West-Side, coffee shop: Picasso and Chagall prints on the wall, and they even had a liquor license.

We went there following a meeting with Bernie Madison. I hadn't liked the way Hannah appeared during our discussion in the lawyer's office. She seemed listless, hardly following when he explained what a "gray area of the law" we were getting into. Bernie tried hard to get us to agree to some sort of mediation but Hannah refused. "I don't want to hear what he has to say. I want him out," she insisted. "Whatever it costs me."

Apparently, that amount of defiance had used up most of Hannah's remaining energy because when we walked from our cars to the restaurant she leaned heavily on my arm.

She isn't that old, I thought. *She's still in her sixties. But she's had more than enough pain for one life and this conflict and uncertainty has to be a terrible burden.*

We sat and studied our menus.

"Let's start with martinis." I suggested. Did you know that the very first martini I ever drank was at your house, served to me by your husband? We'll drink to that grand old man. Maybe that'll revive you a bit."

"Good idea!" Hannah said.

Our drinks came. We relaxed and sipped them slowly.

"Mark," she said, "don't for a moment think that I'm a foolish old woman. I'm not ready to be an old woman, certainly not a foolish old woman. I've still got lots of life left ahead of me. But I don't believe you can grasp the horror of living the way I live. That man's very being is a torture to me; every waking minute. I close myself in my room and I'm no longer sure if I'm in my own house or shut away in Dachau. Everything goes dark. I'm terrified... And I try to pretend this isn't happening. But it is happening. It can't go on this way. It mustn't!"

"Hannah, how is it possible I never noticed before that you have blue eyes? They're very pretty. I'm not trying to change the subject. I just didn't notice them till now."

She looked at me as if I were crazy. In a moment the anger on her face gave way to thoughtfulness.

"Otto used to love my blue eyes. He often would ask me, 'Where does a Jew come off having such blue eyes?' How about Louella? I can't remember what color her eyes are."

"Green."

"It must be hard on you, being apart so much of the time."

"Yes, but it's temporary … I think."

"She's a very special woman, Mark. You must treasure her."

I responded with only a nod of agreement as our waitress arrived with platters of mid-eastern appetizers.

After a period of silence I said, "Hannah, you haven't asked me about how we're getting on with Laura's senior thesis. Do you want me to bring you up to date?"

"Ach, no child. Everywhere I read about Laura. It's amazing what's happening to her. But no, there's enough on my mind today. We'll talk about Laura another time."

Once Laura's name was spoken, I fought an almost irresistible urge to tell Hannah what I had so recently stumbled upon, about Laura and Victor's sexual involvement. It was so tempting to offer Hannah one more thing to use in her damnation of Victor's character, but there was no chance I would betray the trust which had been given me. And then it occurred to me, "Maybe Hannah already knows about their hanky panky. She found out about me and Laura, after all. Maybe Laura told her about being with Victor too?" Anyway, I wasn't going to destroy my working relationship with Laura, not for the sake of passing on gossip.

We finished eating and over Turkish coffee we summed up our afternoon meeting with Bernie.

"So you've empowered him to go ahead, full steam; to do all he can to evict The Quest. Right?"

"Exactly!" she said.

"And he's going to request a jury trial because you, with your blue eyes, are such a sympathetic character and we'll probably have a better chance than if we simply go before a judge.

"Not my blue eyes—justice," she said, standing.

I paid our bill and we went outside. Hannah again surprised me by leaning heavily on my arm. I escorted her to her yellow pick-up-truck and returned to my old Buick.

CHAPTER THIRTY-ONE

THE NEXT morning, after dawdling over fried eggs, freshly squeezed orange juice, and buttered toast, I realized I was going to be late for school. The telephone rang as I was putting on my coat and opening the front door.

No time for that. If it's important they'll leave a message. I'll deal with it in the afternoon.

Before I reached my classroom, Louie stepped out of his office and said, "Phone call, Mark. A woman named Gertrude says it's important you call the farm right away."

"Thanks Louie. Will you check my class. If the student teacher is there, just ask him to get started. He'll be fine. Thanks."

I sat at Louie's desk and dialed the farm. Gertrude answered on the first ring.

"It's me. Mark. What's happening?"

"Hannah," she said. "She's had a stroke. She's in the hospital, in Springfield. She's in intensive care, but they expect her to pull through."

"Tell me more. What happened?"

"Last night, around eight o'clock. I was upstairs, passing Hannah's room and I heard her fall. I went in. She was lying there, unconscious. Victor called the rescue squad. By the time they got here she was awake, but incoherent, unable to stand, and her face was all distorted. I rode with her in the ambulance. Once the doctors took charge Victor came and brought me home. That's just about everything I can tell you."

"Did you talk to her doctors this morning?"

"No."

"All right. I'll call them right now and I can go there after school. Thank you for calling me, Gertrude."

I phoned the hospital and the floor nurse assured me that there was nothing for me to do now. Hannah was resting gently, and she was probably facing a protracted period of intensive physical therapy, but the prognosis was good.

At lunch break I phoned Louella to tell her.

"My God!" Louella said. "Should I come home and take care of her? She doesn't really have anybody else, does she?"

"That's a nice offer, but wait till I see her. Maybe the people at the farm will take care of her, although I'm not sure how they're feeling about her anymore."

I was at the hospital by four in the afternoon.

"She's in her room," I was told, "top floor, room 302." I climbed the steps, two at a time. The floor nurse pointed me to her room. I entered and my trepidation gave way to surprise as I saw Gertrude seated in an armchair, with eight month old Victor Jr. asleep in her arms. Hannah, too, was sleeping. Liquid, either nutrition or medication, or probably both, dripped into her arms from suspended plastic sacks. An oxygen breathing tube pinched off her nose. Otherwise she simply looked as I suppose she always looked when she was asleep.

I surprised myself by bending down to kiss Gertrude on the cheek.

"How is she?" I whispered. "Have you seen her awake yet?"

"I'm told that we don't have to whisper." Gertrude said softly, "But we'll try not to wake the baby. Hannah was awake when I got here, a couple of hours ago. I'm pretty sure that she knew me, but she wasn't able to talk."

"What does her doctor say? Do we know what's happening?"

"Yes and no," Gertrude answered. "It was a stroke on the right side of her brain, which leaves the left side of her body paralyzed. She isn't going to die from it and she may even gain back most of what she's lost. They don't know. They do know that it will be a long process of rehabilitation."

"In the hospital or at home?"

"Both, I'd expect."

Still standing, I gave my attention to Hannah, whose breathing was louder than I had first noticed. With each breath there was a slight grimace accompanied by a curling of the left side of her lips.

I sat down in the remaining, straight backed chair.

"I'm surprised to find you here, Gertrude, and very glad that you came."

"Surprised? You should know better. You can remember Victor saying that 'service to others is what our lives are about.' Can't you?"

"Don't lecture me, Gertrude. Not now, for God's sake."

I regretted those words as soon as they were spoken.

Get a hold on yourself, Mark, She doesn't have to be here, you know!

"I'm sorry, Gertrude. So what happens now? I told of Louella's offer to leave her job, to come here and take care of Hannah."

"We can take care of her," was Gertrude's brusque reply. "There are enough of us on the farm. She's lucky, you know."

I said nothing. After a moment Gertrude's disapproval seemed to soften. She said, "It was very nice of Louella to make the offer. And I'm sure Hannah will appreciate it, whenever she's able to hear of it.... We'll make it work out, somehow."

She stood up, with the baby still in her arms. Victor Jr. opened his eyes and gave just one cry as he surveyed the room.

"One of us will be back tomorrow," Gertrude said, and she left.

I stayed for an hour more. Hannah slept the whole time. The floor nurse, a petite, dark skinned Asian, told me that, "Even if you wait till she wakes, she isn't going to know you're here. She's sedated. Why don't you come back tomorrow?"

That's what I did; the following afternoon.

When I returned to the hospital Hannah was awake. A doctor and the same petite nurse stood by her bed. I tried to make contact with Hannah but she was too disoriented to register that she knew me.

"Are you the next of kin?" asked the attending physician.

"She doesn't have any." I answered. "But I'm the closest she's got to having one. So I'd appreciate it if you could tell me what's happening."

The doctor, whom I assumed was about ten years older than I, scrutinized me for a moment and apparently decided that I was worthy of his opinion.

"It's like this," he said. "You know that a stroke is an interruption of blood flow into the brain. In this case, we believe there was only a single clot causing the interruption and it wasn't of a major size. That's what we think. She is being treated with blood thinners to forestall a recurrence. We'll keep her here for a couple of days rest and by then she should be ready to move into our rehabilitation pavilion. She is going to need a lot of retraining...relearning the basic skills which we take for granted...all of them. How well she does will depend upon how well she works at it, but if she works hard, I don't see why she shouldn't regain most of those skills."

"And when will she be able to go home?"

"Oh, It's too soon to ask that. Maybe in a month. Maybe less. And then she will need someone to watch her and to care for her for quite a while. But let's not rush."

He left the room before I could think of any more questions.

The little nurse fussed with the various tubes attaching Hannah to the hospital. She raised Hannah's head and fluffed up her pillow. She washed Hannah's face with a damp cloth then suggested to me that I might speak with the patient, but I shouldn't expect any response. "Not today, at least."

"Thanks. Thank you for everything. And tell me, please, has she had any other visitors today?"

"Yes, there was a heavy set woman who visited this morning. Same one who was here yesterday; with her baby"

"Thanks."

In the days that followed it appeared that Hannah's stroke was less severe than we feared. Soon she was recognizing faces; mine, Gertrude's, Patty's, Rita's. She had visitors every day and responded positively to company. Speech was hard; she spoke only a few words and these were slurred, nearly incomprehensible. But clearly, Hannah was aware of her surroundings and was making a valiant effort at finding the right words.

When she was released from the hospital, in February, Louella suggested she could take her two weeks vacation time and come home to care for Hannah, despite Gertrude's instance that it wouldn't be necessary, that the inhabitants of the farm were perfectly able to meet all of Hannah's needs.

I passed those words on to Louella, who replied, "Well, I'll come home anyway. I'll spend a couple of hours a day with Hannah and the rest of the time I'll be there with you."

Louella quickly settled into a routine. We ate breakfast together. I went off to school and she drove to the farm. She bathed Hannah and helped her dress. Leaning heavily on her two-wheeled walker Hannah was able to stroll, first around her room, then up and down the hallway. The major project, for the two of them, was conversation. For Hannah speaking was hard work. She had difficulty searching for the words she needed, and difficulty forcing her mouth to form and produce the words once she recalled them. Louella realized that Hannah had a perfect grasp of everything that had happened before her stroke, but that her short term memory was problematic. "Don't let it worry you. The doctor assured you that it will get better. Remember? No, of course you don't remember. If you did remember we wouldn't need to have this conversation, would we?"

Hannah understood and tried to smile, but the smile was more a grimace than a smile.

Often, Gertrude would bring little Victor upstairs to Hannah's room. When Hannah lay down to nap, Gertrude and Louella would sit in the living room and work at reestablishing their nearly abandoned friendship.

One afternoon I returned from school to find Louella already home from the farm. I hung my overcoat in the hall closet. Louella was reaching high into the kitchen cabinets searching out the wine glasses.

"Wine? Now? Just like that? Why the unexpected treat." I asked.

"It's what sophisticated people do. A glass of wine in the afternoon. It's like a ritual."

From the back of the refrigerator Louella extracted a bottle of wine which Hannah had brought to us the last time we had her to supper. I unscrewed the metal cap and poured the two glasses, full, almost to the rim. We settled down on the living room couch.

I took a drink and said, "This could become a very nice habit."

"You're supposed to sip it," my wife said. "Slowly. Taste it on your tongue before you swallow it."

"Okay. Now tell me. How's the patient this afternoon?"

"Hannah's in pretty good shape. She's better every day, making real progress."

"I'll bet it's good for her, having three or four women hovering over her, like she's the queen bee."

"Well yes. But the other thing that's happening, Mark, is that Gertrude and I are becoming friends again. It feels good. You know what she said to me? She reminded me, "I was your maid of honor, Louella. We were so close once. What happened between us?" I think we both felt like crying when she said that... In fact, we may have."

That stopped me. I sipped some more wine and then said, "Be careful, Louella. I'm glad that you're rekindling memories...but you may be entering a place you don't want to go to. Somebody... at least one of you is going to find yourself in an impossible position. It's about loyalties. You're going to find yourself squeezed between Gertrude and Hannah, and it's Victor that will be doing the squeezing. I can see it happening."

"That's nuts, Mark... Or, at least I hope it's nuts. Anyway," Louella added, "Victor won't make any more trouble this week. Gertrude told me he's leaving for Texas tomorrow."

"You mean the commune?"

"Un huh. The same place where Jeremy learned the dance movements. Gertrude says they've developed a meeting of the minds; the two groups. It's like they're comparing and sharing all the time. And she says they really love Victor. So now he's going out there for two weeks. He'll be their guest, a sort of guru-in-residence, I suppose."

"I thought Jeremy was the one Victor sends there, as his representative."

"No, Jeremy went there to learn movements, but now they're inviting Victor to come and instruct them in his teaching methods."

"You mean Victor knows stuff they don't know?"

"Apparently he does. Or at least they think so. Victor is pretty good at what he does, That's what Gertrude tells me, anyway."

"Well, like you said, maybe it's a different place while Victor is away."

CHAPTER THIRTY-TWO

A DAY later, crossing the campus, I saw Al Kramer lumbering towards me. We met and were, at first, unsure how to greet one another. At one time, Al would have embraced me in a bear-hug. Now we shook hands.

"How are you doing, Mark?"

"Good. Thanks..." After a moment, looking into his eyes, I asked, "Are we still friends, Al?"

Instead of answering my question he said, "Your friend Hannah is doing wonderfully, I can tell. I see her every day and every day she gets stronger."

"Right."

"And it's good to have Louella around again. It's been a long time since she's been to the farm. It's nice to have her back."

When I nodded but didn't answer, Al went on, "You know, Mark, this stroke of Hannah's, it's a real game changer. Isn't it?"

"I gotta go Al. I'm late for a meeting. We'll talk about it some time."

And we continued walking in opposite directions. I don't know where Al was heading, but I was on my way to Bernie Madison's law office.

Bernie had phoned, asking me to come over. "I'll bring you up to date and we'll talk about what comes next," he said.

This time, instead of sitting in his office under the gaze of Abraham Lincoln, Bernie escorted me into the parlor. We sat on comfortably upholstered chairs and drank coffee.

Once we were seated Bernie asked me, "So? Is she going to be all right? Is she going to recover? Partially? How much? Does she still want the farm for herself?....Or maybe she's better off dropping the whole case, staying where she is and letting them take care of her for the rest of her life. I hear stories, you know. This isn't a very big town. That's what people are suggesting, and that's what I'd advise her to do. Don't you feel that would be the best thing for her? But I'm only her lawyer. You tell me... Which way you want this to go?"

"Whoa up, Bernie. You're asking me too much at once. Okay. I'll try to answer you. But nobody can say for sure how Hannah's recovery will go. I think she's coming along fine. Her memory's mostly back now. Her speech is getting better. She's getting around with a walker. The doctors say that she should keep improving... I don't know."

"Well, I'm glad for her. Glad it wasn't worse. Now what about the rest of it?"

"Bernie, she wants her farm back.—No, that's not the way to say it.—The farm is hers and she wants all those people to go away, to leave her in peace."

"So Hannah's case continues?"

"I think so, Bernie."

"All right. We've already given them papers notifying them they are trespassing and demanding that they evacuate the premises. It seems they're just going to ignore our first volley. I can request the court to take action, enforce an eviction. But whatever we do, the first step will be all of us getting together in judge's chambers for a discovery of the facts. Shall I set it up for next week? This time Victor will have to appear. His invitation will have the power of a subpoena."

"Well, not yet. Victor's gone out to Texas for a couple of weeks. Can you set it up for when he gets back? I suspect that Hannah will be that much stronger by then."

"I'll do my best. As I told you, my evaluation is that this could go either way. But, all right, let's go for it. I'll set up the court appearance, hopefully somewhere's about three weeks from now."

"You're a good man, Bernie," I said as I gulped the last of my coffee and stood to leave.

*

I drove home, back to our cozy prefab, parked my Buick next to Louella's Bug, and entered. I found Louella sitting still on the living room recliner. She wasn't reading. No music was playing. She just looked at me, holding my gaze for a moment. She gestured that I sit on the couch. "What is it, for God's sake? Something isn't right. That's what you're trying to tell me, isn't it?"

"It's Gertrude," she said. "I went out to be with Hannah this morning, maybe around ten. Hannah looks good, by the way. We were up in her room, talking… Through the window, we saw the limo come to take Victor to the airport."

"Right." I said. "Today's the day he goes out to Texas, as The Quest's ambassador to the West."

"We stayed upstairs all morning. Hannah wanted me to help her do some of her exercises. She's getting so much stronger, you can see her improve from day to day. At lunchtime Rita came over from the Winnebago. She knocked on the door and called out for Hannah to open up. 'I've brought you a tray. It's your lunch.' I opened the door and when she saw me Rita said, 'I didn't know you were here, Louella. Why don't you go down and get yourself some food. I'll sit here with Hannah for a while.' I told her there was no need to stay but she insisted. 'Remember,' she said, 'Service to others is what The Quest is all about.'"

"Louella, you're going somewhere with this story?" I asked. "Right?"

"You listen. I'll talk," she said. She picked up her narrative where I had interrupted.

"Rita's exact words were 'I'm here to serve her. You take some time off, Louella.' So I kissed Hannah and went downstairs to have lunch with whoever was there. I've got to admit, I was more comfortable than otherwise, knowing that Victor was on his way to Texas. I didn't see anybody downstairs so I opened the fridge and helped myself to a plateful of food, and yes, I left money in the box.

I pulled out a bench, sat down and began eating. Then I heard someone coming. It was Gertrude. As soon as she saw me she turned to
go back upstairs. Wait, stop,I said. Then, as she reluctantly came
toward me, I saw her black eye. I got up, of course, and took her in
my arms. Mark, it was terrible."

Louella was sniffling and having difficulty finding the right
word. I held her for a moment and then she continued.

"This wasn't the first time Victor hit me." Gertrude. said. 'He
doesn't hit me very often, but this time.... he claims it was all about
me—or me and you, Mark.' Anyway, it happened when Gertrude was
packing Victor's suitcase, the way she always does before his trips
and while she was packing she made the mistake of telling him not
to worry about how she'd be while he was gone. What she said was
'I'm so happy that I'm becoming friends with Louella again. I'll have
her company while you're away.'"

"That's all she said. Or something like that. But it was enough
to set him off. Victor whirled around and his fist struck her directly
in the face. He accused her of betraying him, of undermining everything that he has done"

"Slow down Louella. Catch your breath." I said. "Did Hannah
know? Did everyone else know that he hits her? They must of."

Louella answered, "Patricia knew that Victor is an abuser. She's
been a comfort to Gertrude. I don't know if Hannah knew or not.
Maybe she felt it or suspected. I don't know. She certainly knows
now, although she's so involved in he own recovery, I doubt that
she's got much time to sympathize with Gertrude's troubles."

"Did you tell Gertrude to take the baby and leave?"

"No, of course not. She still loves the man. I came home to get
you. We're going back to the farm now. You can be with Hannah and
I'm going to sit with Gertrude."

In the car, on our way to the farm, we tried to reconcile our
pictures of Victor, the teacher, with this new Victor, the abuser. It
would have helped clarify our understanding of what drove the man
if I could tell Louella what I inadvertently learned from Victor's

love letter to Laura, but I wasn't ready to pass on information that I considered private: strictly between Laura and me. I couldn't bring myself to speak of Victor's affair with Laura, not even now—not even to my wife.

We arrived at the lane. I slowed the car to a crawl as a new thought bothered me, "Louella, didn't he tell us that we were never to express anger? Of course he did! 'Non- expression of negative emotions,' he called it. That's what gave all of us so much trouble at the beginning. He said that expressing anger only produces more anger. His whole idea, as far as I understood it, was to become awake, be aware of yourself. Just the opposite of what he really is."

"Sure," she answered. "Hitting his woman is as far from the teachings as you could possibly get. I suppose it means that he is being driven by demons that we can't conceive of. I'm not accustomed to thinking of Victor as insecure. He's always so pompous and positive. But, maybe, underneath, he doesn't think that he's amounted to much."

"Maybe," I said. Louella answered "Don't make excuses. I think he's nothing more than a tyrant. He's full of bombast, self-gratification, falsehood, and a whole lot of worse traits I can't think of just now."

Still driving as slowly as I could without stalling the motor, I scanned the barnyard, searching for any of Ruthie's goat friends. None were visible just then.

"Sure." I said, "But doesn't it all add up to insecurity? Look. He was part of the Gurdjief movement in New York and they kicked him out. Didn't they? Everything he's established here on the farm, he's got just because of Hannah's neediness and now he thinks he may be loosing whatever he's accomplished with his life. I'd be pretty insecure in that situation."

"But you wouldn't hit me, would you?"

"Hah! Like I'd have a chance of defending myself if I did!"— Louella took one of my hands from the steering wheel and brought it to her lips.

*

We approached the farmhouse and I pulled up to the front door, the way we used to park when Hannah and Otto were the farm's only inhabitants. These days Victor insisted that visitors pull off to the side of the house, where a parking lot had been cleared and graveled. But Victor wasn't there and I was enjoying my tiny act of defiance.

As we walked in, I had a thought. I didn't want to say it aloud to Louella, but I kept turning over in my mind what a difference this might make to Bernie's case. Somehow, I thought, it ought to strengthen our position—Wouldn't it?

CHAPTER THIRTY-THREE

LOUELLA'S VACATION was just about over and we were breakfasting on bagels and coffee at The Lemon Tree, seated at the same table where Hannah and I sat on the day before her stroke.

"So this is it." I said as I stirred sugar into my coffee mug. "This afternoon you fly out and tomorrow you're back at work."

"Right, Mark. I'll hunker down in my sanctuary while you're playing out your role on the world's stage."

I nodded and sipped the hot, sweet coffee. I was quite aware that I was enjoying the frantic pace of my life, and was proud of being fully used by whatever forces were driving me. I felt both used and tested. It was exciting, meeting the challenge.

Then I became aware that my thought's were veering towards fantasy. *Wake up Mark. Here and now. Pay attention!*

Instantly, I was back with my wife, seated across from me.

"I'll miss you, Louella. Strange.... I will miss you and yet it feels right for you to be going back. I know it won't be forever, and it isn't as if I don't have anything to keep me busy while I wait for you."

She reached across the table top and took one of my hands into hers. "You're silly. You're sweet, but you're hardly a romantic. Are you?"

"What do you mean?"

"Look Mark... I take it back. You're quite romantic enough to suit me. The way I see it, we have a good marriage. It's an unusual set up, and it may look crazy to the rest of the world, but I think it works... So far at least... You're right... I won't stay out there forever. I love you for letting me do what I'm doing; I'm still learning so much. The work I do out there, it's an adventure. I'm having my adventure, and God knows, you're having yours!'"

She let go of my hand, sat back and finished her coffee. We paid, got up and went out into the overcast cold.

"Well, I said, "It isn't as if you were leaving me here and going off to work in California or in Florida. At least if we get snow here, tonight, you'll probably get it tomorrow in New York, my love."

That night, while I was home watching television, the phone rang. It wasn't Louella telling me she had arrived in Peekskill. It was Laura telephoning from Chicago.

"It's me, checking in. How're you guys doing?"

"I'm doing fine Laura. Louella just left; back to New York. She spent most of these two weeks with Hannah. It's amazing how much Hannah's gaining strength. Her speech is still slurred, but you can understand her now. And that's about it. So now it's your turn. Tell me what it's like to be a star performer at all those rallies."

"Star, huh?... Well, the pay stinks, the dressing rooms are filthy, the wardroom and make-up departments are understaffed. But the people are great. This evening they had me addressing a rally at The University of Chicago. Mandel Hall was full. There were people who couldn't get in."

"That sounds exciting."

"Kevin spoke before me. He talked about the history of Viet Nam, about how the French weren't able to win against people fighting for independence and so they asked us to do it for them. Then, before Kevin introduced me, they showed a movie of the newsreel clips from the shooting on campus. Wow!

When I came out to speak the students went wild and, when I finished, two girls came out on the stage and handed me the biggest bouquet of flowers you've ever seen."

"What about your speech, Laura? What did you tell them?"

"Same as always. It's getting pretty routine now. But Kevin had me add something this time. He told me to say something about 'bringing the war home.' He wanted me to say that 'my son, Zachary was the first casualty on American soil, but that he won't be the last one.'"

"Did you say it?"

"Sure."

"So who is this Kevin, anyway?"

"He's sort of like you, Mark. He's my other 'handler.' You're my first. But he's cuter than you, and he isn't married. I'm pretty sure he's dying to get into my undies. He doesn't understand that I don't do that stuff anymore. But he's nice to have around, anyway."

As Laura spoke I visualized the two of us, lying in the hay barn. I was pleased that I had been the one who lay in the hay with her, and not Kevin, whoever he is. *Apparently he isn't going to have that pleasure.* Next my mind flashed to Victor, who, not so long ago, unbeknownst to me, had also been pleasing himself with Laura. I wanted to tell her that Victor was an abuser. Maybe she already knew? *No! I won't be the one to tell her that Victor had just given a black eye to the mother of his own child.*

These thoughts flashed by quickly, not slowing the conversation at all.

"Are you managing to keep up your log and your diary?" I asked.

"Yesss..." she drawled, wearily.

I made a few suggestions, telling her how she might combine the piles of information she was amassing and boil it down into a coherent senior thesis. Somehow, I suspected that Laura wasn't paying much attention to my ideas. *Each time we speak, these days, I sense changes in our relationship. It's not that she's become distant. It's something else. She's become her own person, with her own agenda. Relax, Mark. It's good, what's happening to her.*

Then I sat up in my chair, and in my most professorial voice, I spoke into the receiver; "I hope you aren't counting on me to write your memoirs and your thesis, the same way you're letting this Kevin fellow write your speeches."

"Bah," she replied. You'll do just what you have to do. Same as I will."

"Okay, Laura. Tell me your schedule. Do you know where you'll be going next?"

"Kevin is going to wake me up in time for a rally tomorrow

afternoon. It's at The University of Wisconsin... Let me see... I think there's one other stop on this tour, at a church somewhere, and at the end of the week we fly back to Texas. I'll get to sleep in my own bed again and Kevin has scheduled a couple of appearances right in Dallas."

"Laura, before we call it a night, I need to tell you again how much I admire you for what you are doing. You're great! Really. And I appreciate you."

"You're sweet, Mark."

We said our goodbyes and I hung up the phone happy. Happy to have told her I admired her and how pleased I was with what she was doing: proud that in the face of unspeakable tragedy, instead of giving in to misery, Laura had built a new life for herself. She'd built it around her tragedy. It wasn't a role she had chosen, but she played out the role that was thrust upon her with a strength that astounded me.

I lay down to sleep, but before sleeping I mentally checked off the issues currently in my life. *Louella works in Peekskill, New York and I work in Cold Springs, Ohio yet the separation seems to be okay, for both of us; Hannah, it seems, is being well cared for by the inhabitants of the farm—despite the fact that Bernie has scheduled a hearing in judge's chambers, to take place in three weeks.- or maybe they don't know it yet? No. They are good people. They'd take good care of Hannah in any case. My day job is fine; my work with Laura, as her lifeline to the college is a wondrous thing: good for her and amazingly good for me.*

Contented by the quick summation, I dropped into sleep.

CHAPTER THIRTY-FOUR

SUDDENLY, with no expectation, everything changed.

The alarm was set to ring at six thirty in the morning but moments before that I heard ringing. My feet were on the floor before I realized that it wasn't the alarm. It was the telephone.

It was Louella. All she said was "A horror. Go. Turn on your television and then call me back as soon as you are ready."

I made a necessary stop in the bathroom before proceeding to the living room where I switched on the set, already tuned for "Good Morning America."

First I had to watch a commercial for Florida orange juice.

Then the grim faced news anchor returned to report:

"We are getting more details about last night's murder in Texas. The accused shooter is identified as Laura Steiner, the darling of the antiwar new-left, the popular speaker who has been going from campus to campus, from rally to rally, the same Laura Steiner who less than a year ago tragically had her infant shot to death at the Horace Mann College riot." The woman at his side, the attractive co-anchor interrupted. "Now we have the name of the victim as well. He was Victor Lamotta, also of Cold Springs, Ohio, the very same town in which, you all remember, Laura Steiner's baby was shot to death by National Guardsmen during a student antiwar demonstration at Horace Mann College. There's no word, so far, as to what motivated the shooting."

My stomach reacted before my brain. I was on a jet liner, hitting an air pocket and plunging earthward. Or maybe on an elevator as the cable snapped.

"Victor, Victor..." I thought. "*That wasn't what we wanted to happen. I thought all sorts of evil things about you, called you vile names—but you've been central to my life for nearly as long as I've been here in Ohio. You've taught me so much. You didn't deserve to die!"*

Then I thought of Laura. *How could this be? Poor, poor Laura. What crazy thing have you done? Why, for God's sake?*

I knew they were both in Texas, Laura at home and Victor at the commune. That was all I knew.

I remembered Al Kramer's comment that Hannah's stroke would turn out to be "a game changer."

"Hah," I thought. "This is the real game changer!"

Mechanically, I dialed Louella's number.

"Hello. Mark?"

"That's a hell of a thing to wake up to, Louella. I'm stunned. Now what am I supposed to do?"

"I have no idea what you're supposed to do. But you'll figure it out. Right now it isn't about you, Mark. It's about poor Laura. Have you any idea why she did it?"

"No....yes, I'm beginning to.... An idea, but only the vaguest sort of idea. Louella, I guess I still have to teach school today. Maybe by this afternoon we'll know something and then it will be clearer what I should do. Poor Laura! I don't even know how to get in touch with her. Do you think the police will let me talk to her?"

"Try. But I think you're right, Mark. We'll each go to work and we'll talk later, as soon as we know what really happened. Wait. No, I don't think they'll let you talk to her. Why don't you call Bernie Madison? Maybe he'll know how one gets in touch with somebody who's in police custody."

"I love you, Louella. We'll talk later."

"Love you too," she said. "Be strong. I'll see if I can raise Gertrude on the phone. She must be distraught. I'll see if I can be of any help at this distance."

I dressed, drank coffee, skipped breakfast, and went off to school.

I was astounded at how normal everything felt. The day started out, as usual, with "show and tell." The class already knew about the shooting. Apparently, all their parents started their mornings with the news programs. My kids were eager to share tidbits about our town once again becoming the center of nationwide attention. I didn't allow us to dwell overlong on the shooting and we moved on to story writing. I wrote a number of words on the blackboard and asked the students each to incorporate them into a made up story. "Later, we'll share your stories and critique them as well."

"*How can it be?*" I thought. "*My world turns upside down and yet my world continues as if nothing is changed.*"

Sometime in the mid-morning my principal, Louie came into my classroom and said, "Mark, I'll take your class for the rest of the day. You're expected at Dean Lacy's office, right away."

Walking into Tom Lacy's familiar office I was happy to see Bernie Madison was also there, puffing on a cigarette.

"Hello Mark." Tom said. "Do you know Bernie Madison, attorney for the college?"

"Sure, I do. Hi Bernie. But I've been in class all morning. Any fresh news? Have you heard anything that isn't on the television yet?"

Tom motioned me to sit. Bernie answered me. "I made a few telephone calls. Apparently it was some sort of love spat. Laura says it was self defense, that Lamotta tried to rape her."

"Do you know where it happened?"

"I do." Bernie answered. "It was at some sort of new-age commune, outside of Dallas. Laura gave a talk there last night. They were putting her up for the night and it happened in her cabin. We don't know why Victor Lamotta was there and we don't know why she let him into her room."

Now Tom spoke up for the first time. He asked, "Do you know anything we don't know, Mark?"

I closed my eyes for an instant and breathed deeply, wondering how much to tell them.

"Yes." I answered. "They used to be lovers—back when Laura lived out at the farm. She was one of his followers...his student, and they were sleeping together, on the side."

"Interesting," Tom said. "How did you know that?"

"I didn't know until recently when Laura gave me a pile of her correspondence to read. I'm still not sure if she wanted me to read that particular letter or not."

Bernie leaned over the coffee table, strewn with college brochures, reached for an ash tray and stubbed out his cigarette. "I thought I'd quit these damn things. Maybe later. Anyway Mark, here's what we're thinking. This is going to be a messy story. The media will undoubtedly pick it up and run with it for as long as they can keep it alive.... Our job is to minimize whatever connections they make to the college. There's no way we can keep Horace Mann College out of the story. It's already part of what everybody thinks of when they hear Laura's name. But at least we can try to minimize the damage."

Bernie paused to light another cigarette and then continued, "The college is sending me out to Dallas tonight. They want me to go there and figure out what I might do to mitigate the harm being done to Horace Mann, the institution that employs both of us. And they want you to come with me. It seems you're the person here who knows Laura best, who's closest to her. We're sure you can help."

Now Tom joined in. "Mark, she likes you, she trusts you. You'll be the one to introduce her to Bernie. To see that she accepts his help."

My mind raced. *Do I tell them that Laura and I were once lovers, apparently at the same time that she and Victor were sleeping together? ... No. If that became known the story would become even more lurid ...I visualized the headlines:'killer had been sleeping with two married men'.*

All I said was "I'm yours to command."

"Good." Tom said. "You'll both see what you can do for Laura. But the purpose of your being there is to protect our already damaged reputation, to keep us out of the story as far as you are able. Remember that, and we'll talk every day. And Mark, Louie will be covering your classes. Don't worry about a thing. It will be up to the two of you to decide how long you should stay; as long as you feel it's useful. The college will be covering your expenses."

Within the hour, Bernie and I were on our way to the Cincinnati airport, chauffeured in the President's Cadillac.

CHAPTER THIRTY-FIVE

WE WERE in Dallas early in the afternoon and taxied directly from the airport to the Women's House of Detention where a stocky policeman seated at the entrance asked us our business. Bernie, introduced himself as Laura's lawyer and was admitted, but only after he produced identification as well as a letter from President, Jim Hillestad.

I was refused admission. "You got no right to go in there." he said. I remained, waiting on a hard wooden bench, for the next forty-five minutes until Bernie emerged.

He didn't tell me much during the taxi ride to our hotel. I assumed he didn't want to talk in front of our taxi driver. We checked into our separate rooms and then met in the bar. We each got a beer and a saucer of salty bar snacks which we carried to a dark but comfortable nook.

"OK, now I can tell you everything," Bernie began. "This, being the enlightened state of Texas, Laura is charged with first degree willful murder. Willful murder carries a death sentence."

"But..." I couldn't find the thought I was going to express. *"Death sentence!"* I shuddered. Not for a moment had the possibility of a death sentence occurred to me.

"Let me go on," Bernie said. "We talked for a long time and..."

"No, before you tell me what you talked about, tell me how she is. Is she holding herself together? How does she look?"

"You've got to realize, Mark, this is the first time I've met her. She seemed strong, worried, confused, healthy...a bit defiant. I've got no idea how this is affecting her because I didn't know her before. But here's the way it went. First, I told her that you and I are sent here by the college, and by the way, Laura is very happy to know that you are here, even if you can't see her. She begged me to take on her defense. She doesn't trust any Dallas lawyer to be on her side."

"Did you agree?"

"Yes—sort of—for now. But she'll have to take a local lawyer as well. I'm not licensed to practice in Texas and even if I was, I wouldn't have any feeling for these people."

Bernie paused, sipped his beer and ate a handful of salted goodies.

"Anyway, here's the way it all happened, according to Laura."

"It turns out that she and our deceased, Victor Lamotta, had been having an affair for quite a while. Right up to the time of the campus riot. I asked her if it stopped then and she volunteered the information that she hasn't slept with anyone since her son was killed."

I suspected that in time it might be important for Bernie to know that I too had been intimate with Laura. But not now. For now I remained silent.

Bernie went on.

"According to Laura, Victor had a longstanding relationship with the commune here in Texas. He comes out here a couple of times a year.... or, I should say he used to come here. Laura doesn't think it was a coincidence, their being here at the same time. She thinks Victor arranged it, that they'd invite her the same time he'd be coming. So she gave her talk and led a discussion about the war. Then she went out to the cabin they gave her for the night. Apparently there are cabins all over the place, isolated, where nobody was likely to hear her if she yelled. Victor showed up later."

"Was he at her talk?" I asked.

"No. She says she had no idea he was in Texas. Not till he knocks on her door and says 'Let me in sweetie, it's Victor.' Well she recognizes his voice and lets him in. She asks what he's doing at the commune and he tells her he's there to lecture too. Then, before you know it, he makes his move. His hands are all over her. She tries to tell him, in her words, 'I don't do that anymore.' But, hey, when a guy's in heat, it takes more than words to turn him off; he's pretty much under the control of his pecker. At this point he's attacking her sexually. Pretty soon she's pinned down on the bed and he's pulling off her clothes. Then Laura figures it out. 'OK, we'll do it,' she says, 'Just like in old times. Let me up and I'll put in my diaphragm.' So he lets her up, and she goes and gets her gun and shoots him. That's the way she tells it. Maybe nobody would of heard her scream, but they certainly heard the shots and they came right away."

"Poor Laura."

"Yeah.... the rest of it's in the newspapers and on television. They're having a field day with this one. It's the juiciest shooting in Dallas since President Kennedy two years ago. Maybe juicier. 'Commie-hippie gunslinger shoots lover' kind of thing."

I felt my stomach churning, so when Bernie suggested we go to the dining room and get something to eat, I declined.

"You go, Bernie. I'm going to my room, take a shower and try to watch the TV coverage you're talking about."

"You won't have any trouble finding it. I'll come up to your room later and we'll plan what comes next. Okay?"

"Sure Bernie."

Thirty minutes later he knocked on my door.

"It's open Bernie, come on in."

I opened the mini bar and extracted two little bottles of gin. Taking two water glasses from the bathroom, I poured for each of us.

"Ice." Bernie said. "This stuff's no good without ice."

"Okay, be calm. The machine's right by the elevator. I'll go."

I returned with a bucket of ice, took my seat again, and said, "Bernie, I feel stupid, sitting around here and being of no help at all. Was it a mistake, my coming with you? What do you really think? I'm not any use to you, am I?"

"Well, you mix up a good drink. Other than that, you may be right. Let's give it a couple of days, though. It certainly calms Laura, knowing you're here, even if they won't let you in to see her. I'll nose around the courts and see if there's some way of getting you in there. Let's see what happens."

We finished our drinks and parted for the night.

In the morning I told Bernie that I would use the day to visit with Laura's parents. "We have a pretty good relationship. Maybe they'll have some ideas worth hearing.

As my taxi approached the Steiner's ranch home there was a familiar sight—television crews and reporters, and curious idlers, camped out on the lawn.

It's been six short months since those vultures disappeared. It's no pleasure to see them again.

Mr. and Mrs. Steiner hurriedly pulled me through the doorway, re-locked the door, and then embraced me.

Their television set, blaring news in the background, masked any sounds from out on the lawn.

Mr. Steiner, as usual wore a business suit, but his face showed three days growth of beard. Mrs. Steiner, wore a plaid housecoat. Her normally, well tended hair was disheveled. She practically pushed me down, onto the couch, and then standing in front of me, her words came, shouted out through tears: "How dare they hold her in jail? The man tried to rape her. That's self defense. Self defense isn't a crime in the state of Texas, is it?—Oh God. Is it Mark?"

She shook her head vehemently, straightened up, and said, "Stay there Mark. I'll make us all a pot of coffee."

We talked for a long time. As it turned out, they didn't have any idea what to do—nor what Bernie or I might do.

I told them what little I had learned from Bernie. They told me they had spoken to Laura twice since her arrest but they weren't allowed to see her either. Of course they were upset, but equally they were confused. Mrs. Steiner kept repeating, "Self defense," and, "After everything that's happened to her, How is this possible?"

"it's possible," I answered, "Because there are a lot of angry rednecks out there who don't like the speeches your daughter's been making. I wish I could tell you what's going to happen. I can't."

When we had voiced our concerns and unhappiness Mr. Steiner offered to drive me back to my hotel.

"You won't have to face the reporters out there. We'll go out through the garage. If they're standing in the driveway, in the way of my Cadillac, let that be their lookout."

Later, in the afternoon, Bernie returned to our hotel. We met in the bar, making ourselves comfortable in our now familiar nook. Bernie told me he had found a local attorney with whom he would share Laura's defense.

"His name is Jackson. Stephen Jackson. He's been around for a long time, mostly doing union work and recently getting involved in what they're calling 'The Civil Rights Movement.' He's not too worried about where his fees are going to come from. He says, 'One way or another, we'll find the money.' What worries him is the nasty state of public opinion in this town. He says we're going to have our hands full."

"You're doing good Bernie. That's progress. Now let me tell you about my visit with Laura's parents."

After I reported on my visit, and the fact that the Steiners had no immediate contributions towards Laura's defense, it occurred to me that I'd best tell Bernie as much as I could—to better acquaint him with his defendant.

"Let me to tell you everything I can about the woman."

I surprised myself by calling her a woman, rather than "a girl." I wasn't sure from where the word just popped out, but in the long disquisition which followed I did my best to describe Laura Steiner, the ill-fated Laura for whom I now had so much respect.

I told Bernie almost everything I could remember about her: everything except that she and I had been intimate. "*Thank God,*" I said to myself, "*I did confess to Louella. The admission hurt my wife terribly. Where would I be today if I hadn't admitted it? I'd be terrified that at any moment it would be revealed—Louella would find out. She'd be through with me. I'd be destroyed. Now it isn't about me and Louella any more. It's all about poor Laura.*"

Bernie and I remained in the bar till nearly midnight.

I spent five more days in Dallas, each day attempting to see

Laura and each day meeting with rebuff. I visited the Steiners a couple of times. I became a sightseer and in the warm March sunshine I explored Dealey Plaza, the grassy knoll and the Book Depository. Mostly I looked forward to my evenings with Bernie when he would inform me of whatever progress he and Stephen Jackson were making, preparing Laura's defense.

On the seventh day, feeling upset with myself superfluous, ineffectual and bored, I wished Bernie "Good luck," asked him "Give my deepest love to Laura," and departed, returning to Cold Springs.

CHAPTER THIRTY-SIX

I WAS relieved to be back in Cold Springs, preparing lessons, teaching, cooking for myself and cleaning the house. Daily phone calls to Bernie kept me up to date with Laura's case. Daily phone calls to my wife in Peekskill helped keep perspective on the unfolding events.

As to Hannah's claim on her house, nothing was settled. The judicial hearing in the judge's chambers, at which we intended to present our case for removing Victor and his followers from the farm, was postponed indefinitely. Neither Hannah nor I knew what her next step should be.

Victor's body had finally been released by the State of Texas, embalmed and flown back to Ohio, where it lay in Copeland's Funeral Home, awaiting the burial service to be held on the weekend.

Waiting to let things sort themselves out was the only course of action I saw for myself.

As for Laura's senior thesis, of which I was the advisor and facilitator, that too was a non-issue. Laura was on trial for her life. She certainly wasn't able to concern herself with whatever public record we were trying to produce. The nightly hour which I used to spend on the telephone with Laura I now used to write in a journal of my own, keeping the record of Laura's saga as up to date as I could.

My first evening back Louella telephoned to say that she would be home in time to attend Victor's funeral. "I never had any love for Victor," she said. "But I know Gertrude is grieving and I want to be there for her."

"What plane should I meet?"

"No, I'm going to drive myself. I'll explain later. I've got so much to tell you! The funeral's the day after tomorrow, right? I'll be driving part of the way tonight, but I promise I won't drive straight through. I'll sleep over, maybe in Pennsylvania and I'll see you tomorrow."

"Well, this is a nice surprise."

The next day I went off to school, expecting Louella to arrive some time in the afternoon. The school day finished and I went home, opened a bottle of beer and sat in the living room awaiting my wife. I sat in front of the blaring television, on which news commentators incessantly repeated whatever facts they could discover about Laura, the late Victor Lamotta, and the commune in Cold Springs, Ohio. Before the bottle was empty I heard Louella's Volkswagen rearranging the gravel in our driveway. I jumped up and went out to greet her. Louella unfolded herself from the car seat, stretched her arms and then embraced and kissed me. It was a quick embrace, which I broke off because my attention was diverted by the boxes, suitcases, loose clothing and shoes that were crammed into her Volkswagen.

"What's going on?"

"I'm home to stay," she answered. "I hope you like the idea."

"You mean you quit your job? Just like that? No. Of course I like it. But why?"

"Let's go inside. I'll explain.—Wait. Help me. Carry in these bags of food. They've been too long in the car already."

We carried in a couple of food bags and Louella put the perishables into our practically empty refrigerator. Then we settled in the living room.

"Well?"

"It's like this," Louella said. "Do you want the short version or the long version?"

"Don't be coy. Just tell me what's happening. Are you okay?"

"I'm fine. And I wasn't fired. On the contrary. We're working on such exciting stuff. I can't wait to tell you all about it. The short version is that anything I produce while I'm working for IBM will belong to IBM and not to me. If I come back to the college I can teach and do my own work on my own time. I'll be able to work on whatever I want to and anything I come up with is going to be mine."

"Are you on the verge of some great discovery? Are you going to make us rich?"

"Don't laugh at me. It could happen. Things are moving so fast now. At IBM they're all hung up on their mainframes and they can't see that the future is in small, individual computers, so small that you can put one on top of your writing desk. Do you remember how excited you were when you got your IBM Selectric typewriter? You didn't need "whiteout" to correct your mistakes any more. All you had to do was type right over them. Well, very soon your Selectric's going to be outmoded. You'll throw it away and be writing with your very own electronic computer."

Louella stood up from couch, and began pacing with excitement, gesturing broadly with her outstretched arms.

"Remember the first time you visited me in Peekskill? I took you inside of the machine they'd just developed. It took up an entire room. Well computers are getting smaller and smaller and pretty soon the little computer I'm talking about will be able to do more than that huge main frame could do, but it wont be any bigger than my suitcase over there."

"Okay," I interrupted, "But what's that got to do with your sudden decision to quit?"

"It's what I've been working on. I've got lots of ideas about how to simplify the way you can talk to your machine. Right now you have to know a complicated set of instructions—a whole different language. But I think I'm coming up with something simpler. It's very exciting!"

"But why now?"

"I guess Victor's service was the trigger...oops, that wasn't a good choice of words, was it? His funeral was the catalyst for something I'd been brooding on for a while.—You know, I'm not even sure that the college will take me back. But I think that they will.—Yeh, I guess it was a pretty sudden decision."

"Don't you have to give two weeks notice or anything?"

"I told them I was leaving to go to a funeral. I'll let them know I'm not coming back. I have enough sick time accumulated so it won't be a problem."

"Really! How about that! I'm very happy."

A thought popped into my mind. *Be aware Mark. This is important, what's happening. Wake up. Be conscious of what you are feeling, seeing and hearing. Be conscious that you are the one who is feeling, seeing and hearing.*

I became aware. It was the sort of self re-collection that Victor wanted us to practice all the time. The thought passed quickly and then I was back in the midst of my reunion with Louella.

"Well, you certainly picked an interesting time to come back. Welcome home, my love. I was sure you'd come back, sooner or later. Hallelujah, you chose sooner! It's going to be wonderful to have you next to me in our bed tonight."

The day of the funeral service held a foretaste of the approaching spring. The temperature climbed to the mid fifties, which meant that the scattered piles of remaining snow were melting at their edges. Sap was rising in the sugar maples, and from the wetlands, behind Copeland's Funeral Home, a few frogs could be heard calling one another. It wasn't spring yet, but it was easy to fool yourself into believing that winter was over.

When I arrived for the eleven o'clock service Copeland's was already crowded. Apparently most of Victor's followers, even some who had not been part of The Quest for years, came for his funeral. *Maybe half of them are here just to feed off the juicy scandal."*

Cora, the woman to whom Victor, until his death, had been lawfully wed, sat at one end of the front row. Next to her sat their two teen aged sons. Next to them were Patricia and Jeremy, then Al and Rita, and at the other end of the row, Gertrude and Louella. I found a seat in the second row, right behind my wife, who had left home early to be with Gertrude. Gertrude's baby, Victor Junior was back at the farm, in the care of Hannah and a baby sitter who could attend to the needs of the eight month old baby if Hannah should become overly tired.

I joined the line of people walking past the open casket. Victor, his eyes closed, appeared to be deep in thought, as though he were about to come out with one of his pronouncements. On either side of the casket were several bouquets. I noted one from Dallas, sent by Bernie Madison. The card read 'I hate to win a case this way.' I wondered if Bernie's gesture was or wasn't in good taste, particularly since the matter of evicting The Quest was far from settled. Well, it was certainly consistent with his New York style.

I took my seat and waited to see what would be said. After all, no matter what words were about to be spoken, when a man is shot to death with his pants off, no matter what gets said, that lurid picture is going to be uppermost in everybody's imagination.

The religious part of the ceremony was conducted by a priest, representing the faith into which Victor had been born but which he had long forsaken. Then Quinten Copeland, the funeral director, asked if there were any in the audience who wanted to comment on Victor's life.

Jeremy was the first to speak.

My attitude towards the pudgy, balding lawyer had changed several times in the few years I'd known him. When he taught the dance movements I found him tedious. When he left his profession to help his wife, Patricia, open the school in Hannah's barn I was impressed by the energy he brought to the job. Then, when he took on the task of defending Victor against Bernie and Hannah's suit I saw him as an enemy. Now I tried to listen to him without prejudgement.

"It is good to see so many of you here," Jeremy began. "Such a large part of our lives has been torn from us. I'm not going to pretend it wasn't a ghastly end to a complicated life. It was. But it was a life dedicated to serving each of us, enabling each of us to become the complete person which is our birthright. Victor taught each of us to awaken, to live consciously, to become real persons. Sometimes he taught by example. Sometimes he may have failed to embody his own teachings. Cora Lamotta, Jake and Sam... Your husband, your father, he was a complex person. Certainly he chal-lenged your patience and your understanding. But look around at the people in this room and know that the legacy he left behind includes having enriched the lives of so many people...No, not so much enriching their lives.... uncovering for them the undiscovered riches already contained within them."

Jeramy paused and then turned toward Gertrude.

"Gertrude, you are left with another treasure—little Victor Junior, whom I know you will cherish. He will grow to know that his father embodied all the contradictions that life presents. And while Victor may not have mastered his own path through those contra-dictions, he helped so many of us to become aware of the choices we make in our lives every waking moment. One more thought for you, in Victor's family. I know it will be hard at first, but my fondest hope is that, in time, there will be a meaningful relationship between Victor's sons: Jake, Sam and little Victor"

I was pleased with Jeramy's words. Now he asked the audience:

"Is there anyone amongst you who would like to tell how your life has been touched by Victor's?"

The first person to address us was a third year student, a trim girl with the grace of a dancer. She had been in my beginner's class for a while before advancing into one of Victor's groups.

"I just want to share one story," she began. "Every time I look in the mirror I'm going to remember the story Victor told us, about how we are born knowing and remembering all that we need to know: past lives, the meaning of life, what is expected of us—all that stuff. But before we learn to speak an angel visits us, each and every one of us. The angel puts his forefinger on our lips and says, 'Shhh. Don't tell anybody what you know. Don't even remember all of it.' And we do forget the knowledge we were born with. All that's left is that concavity above our lips, where the angel pressed his finger. That's the first thing I see when I look in the mirror every morning. Thank you, Victor."

As she returned to her seat I involuntarily pictured Victor, in one of his private sessions with her, lightly pressing his finger to her lips to illustrate his story. Was he sleeping with her?

Several others spoke and then we drove to the cemetery.

Following interment, mourners were invited to the farm to partake in refreshments. Victor's wife and two sons declined. Hannah stayed upstairs in her room. Louella and I remained until all the visitors had gone. We helped clear the trash and clean the dishes. We went upstairs to say good night to Hannah.

It was dark by the time we got home. The temperature was dropping and the sky threatened snow. We settled in the living room.

"So tell me, Louella, is Gertrude going to be all right? What's she thinking?"

"Devastated. Is that the right word?...She doesn't have anything... except for an eight month old baby. That's all that Victor left her. She's just another unwed mother. She's not even sure that she has a place to be. It's a mess, Mark."

"Bummer." I said, walking across to where my wife was sitting. I knelt to the floor in front of her, put my head in her lap, my arms around her legs. After a moment, I looked up and said, "I'm so glad you're home to stay, Louella."

CHAPTER THIRTY-SEVEN

LOUELLA'S FELLOW mathematicians welcomed her back. No salary was available, but she was taken into the fold. She coached students who needed remedial work as well as those who wanted to advance beyond standard course offerings. She was given desk space and made to feel at home. And she was assured that, in a few months, when the next term begins there would be a full-time position available and it was hers for the asking.

"Apparently," she said, "they're still in awe of me because I've been right there, on the cutting edge, while they see themselves as Midwesterners: a lesser breed of mathematician so to speak."

A letter came from Jim Krikun, my old roommate.

Yo, old pal. How did we manage to lose track of each other so completely? Only four years ago I was your best man. You do remember me, don't you? (Just joking) Anyway, I'm doing fine up here in Cleveland. I've got a job in the newspaper business—sort of. I put together give-aways, neighborhood gossip sheets with lots of ads. You can pick up the paper at your shopping market for free. I'm doing pretty good so far.

It's not so good on the dating scene. I've met a few interesting women, but after Horace Mann College...What can I say? Don't you have the feeling that you're sorry for anyone who hasn't had the privilege of spending some time in Cold Springs? What is there to talk about with anyone who hasn't been there?

So here's why I'm writing now—I want to ask you, What's with Gertrude? You and Louella are still in touch with her, aren't you? I've read all about her in the newspaper, of course. Who hasn't? But how is she taking it? Do you think she'd like me to call her? I'd really like to give her some support, even though she left me so abruptly and ferociously after your wedding. I guess she and Victor were a thing already. So let me know what she's thinking, old friend.

Thanks,

Jim

Reading the letter, I felt guilt, even shame, at having completely neglected Jim since he moved to Cleveland. I then read it aloud to Louella.

"What do you think?" I asked.

"The way that I hear it," she replied, "I suspect that Jim wouldn't mind in the least if we showed it to Gertrude. I'm sure that's what he's hoping we'd do."

"Okay," I said. "But she broke his heart once, already. Jim's a nice guy, but he's no match for Gertrude, is he?"

"Well, we'll see. She liked him once, after all. And God knows she needs somebody to care about her right now. Give it to me. I'm going to go talk with Gertrude right now. If I'm not back in time for supper, you'll find something in the fridge. Okay?"

Bernie telephoned daily to report on developments in Laura's trial. It wasn't as though I didn't already know most of what he told me by reading the newspapers or watching television but I was grateful to feel that Bernie still considered me a participant, that he valued my opinions, and he likes having me communicate with Laura,—not directly, but through him.

From Bernie, I learned that Steve Jackson made a motion to change the trial's venue—anywhere other than Dallas. "Dallas," he told the judge, "is still reeling from the shocks it has sustained. Not just from the murders of Kennedy, Tippett, and Oswald," he said. "This is the city where our United Nations representative, Adlai Stevenson, was surrounded by a hissing mob, spat upon and hit on the head with a placard. This is the city where our President, Lyndon Johnson, when he was Vice President, was similarly treated. It is a city full of anger and self-doubt. Now that anger is being inflamed by the press, by seizing on Laura Steiner's opposition to the Vietnam war and identifying her as one of America's enemies. I don't believe that an unbiased jury can be found in this city."

It was a strong appeal, as Bernie described it. Nonetheless, Jackson's motion to transfer the trial's venue was rejected.

Jury selection began. Bernie told me, "We're having a devil of a time figuring out the profile that we're looking for. Thanks be to God for Steve. He's lived here all his life and he knows these people. But he's just as puzzled as I am. Will women be more sympathetic jurors than men? Who knows? The mobs that spat on Johnson and on Stevenson, they were mostly women. We'll have to see."

We spoke again the following day.

"So how goes the jury selection? I asked.

"Almost there," he answered. "I'm learning so much about this crazy city. It turns out that Dallas is the murder capital of the country. No kidding. Well, if a woman murders her husband, that's no big deal and you can bet your house on it, she's going to get off. Same for a man who shoots another man whom he suspects of messing with his wife. Even a plea of 'temporary insanity' has a pretty good chance here. But now, Laura Steiner shoots Victor Lamotta and it's a completely new story. All the rules are different. 'Slut commie shoots her teacher in cold blood.' Here's what scares me, Mark, under Texas law it's the jury that decides what the penalty will be. That's gotta be in our minds, too, as we select the jurors."

"Okay Bernie. I know you guys are doing your very best. Hang in there. And tell Laura that I do love her still."

"Seriously?"

"Come on Bernie. Not that way... Yeah. I do. She's gone off the deep end this time, but life's pushed her, wouldn't you agree?"

"We'll save her, buddy. You give my best to Cold Springs."

"So long, Bernie."

Hearing me replace the receiver, Louella joined me in the living room.

"That was a heck of a long phone call, Mark. Did Bernie have any good news to share?"

"Hardly. His words are optimistic, but I suspect that's not what he's really feeling."

We sat together on the couch and I reported. "Here's the gist of what he's up against. Self defense, particularly defense against attempted rape, seems like a pretty strong case, simple enough to defend. But this is an angry time, and as Bernie said, Dallas is an angry city. Can you believe this? A group of women forced the art museum to get rid of its Picasso paintings because he's a red! That's where he's got to defend a Laura Steiner!"

CHAPTER THIRTY-EIGHT

THE JURY was selected: eight women and four men. The trial opened and was televised nationally. I left my Lab School class in the care of my student teacher while Louella and I stayed home to watch.

Caleb Arnold, prosecutor for The State of Texas, rose to make his presentation to the jury. Solidly built, tall and graying, he appeared to be in his fifties. With an open hand, he half waved at the judge, then he seemed to catch himself and switched his gaze toward the jury. He smiled warmly, looking into the face of each of the jurors.

He spoke in measured phrases, with long pauses.

"My fellow citizens of Dallas," he began. "I have good news to bring you. This trial is going to be brief. Very brief. You've already been in this courthouse for three days, and we thank you for that. I promise, you're not going to have to listen to but a couple of witnesses. And you won't even have any difficult decisions to make because this is a very simple trial."

"What we have here is a rabble rousing leader of the draft card burners who came out to Dallas to spread her anti-American message of hate. She got here, she got re-involved with a fellow she used to sleep with and when things became too hot between them, instead of telling him 'no' what she did was to shoot him three times. This isn't in contention. Laura Steiner—right over there, that's her— admits to all of this."

The cameras swung around to focus on Laura. She was neatly dressed in a white blouse and a dark jacket and skirt. The broadcast wasn't in color, and even if it had been, nobody I knew owned one of those new color television sets, but I had seen the outfit before and knew that the jacket and skirt were dark blue.

I had no idea of what she was feeling. She sat still, impassive. For all that I could see she might just as well be in her doctor's waiting room, with several other patients still ahead of her.

"Now pay attention," said Arnold.

I responded to Arnold's words. My reflections ceased and I sat up straight.

"All I am gonna ask of you is to declare that what this person did was extreme, that she knew what she was doing, and that she did more than she had to do, given the circumstances. It's one thing to make a man leave you be. It's entirely another thing, once he's let you be, to intentionally shoot him dead."

"I'll be counting on your intelligence."

He sat down and Stephen Jackson came forward to present his case for the defense. Jackson wasn't as imposing a man as Arnold. He was of medium height and perhaps ten years younger than the prosecutor. He wore a well fitting suit. From my first look at the man, I felt confidence in him.

He didn't hesitate, but immediately stepped forward and began to speak, clearly and rapidly, yet in a carefully practiced Texas drawl.

"Hello—First of all, I want to correct a misunderstanding you may have got from the prosecution. I hope you all realize that, right now, here in this court, we are not trying some foreign agitator. Not even a New Yorker or an Easterner. Far from it. Laura was born and raised right here in Dallas, just as most of you were. Just as I was. When I was studying for the bar, right here at SMU, Laura was finishing grade school in Turtle Creek. Some of you may have purchased your first Ford automobile from Laura's daddy."

"Okay. Now that we've remembered who it is that's on trial here, I have some agreement with the Prosecutor. This is a very simple case. The defendant is actually the victim. She protected herself from rape. It's as simple as that."

"Fortunately, here in the state of Texas, the right of a woman to defend herself from attack is a basic and a long-honored tradition. Actually, I'm not even sure why it was necessary to bring this woman to trial. Normally, in cases like this, don't we allow the poor woman to go home, be free, and try to rid herself of the horrible memory of what's happened to her?"

"I'm counting on you good people to uphold our tradition of justice and fair play. Thank you."

While Jackson was returning to his seat Louella turned to me and said,

"She does have a chance! Doesn't she? I think his arguments would convince me."

"Shush, I said. "Let's see what happens next."

The judge announced that there were only two witnesses. "The first witness for the prosecution, I call to the stand Thelma Fell."

The tall woman who strode up to the stand was in her late fifties. Her once blond hair was mostly gray and was tied back in a bun. She wore a simple print dress which reached to her ankles.

Thelma Fell was sworn in and then Caleb Arnold began:

"Is it correct that you are a member of the new-age commune where the killing of Victor Lamotta took place?"

"I guess I am. That's not what we call our community, but OK."

"And is it correct that you and your husband occupy the cabin which is nearest to the guest cottage where Laura Steiner was staying?"

"Yes, her cottage is perhaps fifty yards down the path from ours. It's the very last one."

"Thank you. You and your husband, I believe, were the first people to go to that cottage after the shooting. Could you please tell the court what you found there?"

Mrs. Fell spoke clearly, with no hesitation. It was clear, from her accent, that Texas was not her native state. Possibly New England, I thought.

"My husband and I were preparing for bed. We were startled by the sound of three shots and my husband said we'd better go see what happened. We put on bathrobes, took a flashlight, and walked carefully down the path, holding hands. When we got to the cottage I peeked through the window and saw that woman, over there, sitting on the side of the bed. She was crying. We went in. The door wasn't locked."

"Did you know who she was?"

"Yes. She's the one we invited to come talk to us about the war. She was against it."

"Did you attend her talk?"

"No. We didn't. I couldn't understand why she had been invited because we at the commune don't think that politics is the way to get in touch with reality. It's pretty much a side show. We try to work on ourselves and leave politics to the politicians and the rabble rousers.

"And now tell us what you saw when you went into the cottage."

"I told you already. Laura Steiner was sitting on the bed crying. She wasn't wearing very much. Just a brassiere and panties. Victor Lamotta was on the floor, almost at her feet. There was lots of blood all over the place."

"Anything else, Mrs. Fell?"

"Oh, yes, and there was a pistol, lying there on the floor, next to him."

"Did you know Victor Lamotta?"

"Sure. He was one of our teachers. He comes pretty often, from his own school, in Ohio, I believe."

"What did Lamotta have on?"

"Nothing. Maybe his tee shirt, but no pants."

"And what happened next?"

"My husband took off his bathrobe and put it around that woman. Next he called the police. First thing I knew there were lots of others in the room."

"And did Laura Steiner say anything?"

"Not a word. Not one word. She just cried. Or when she wasn't crying she was sniffling. She seemed awfully upset to me."

"Thank you Mrs. Fell. No other questions, your honor."

*

The judge asked Stephen Jackson if he wanted to cross examine the witness.

"No your honor, the defense has no questions for this witness."

The next witness was for the defense. Louella was surprised to see Rita Robbins called to the stand. I wasn't surprised, just pleased. I had suggested to Bernie that one of the people living on the farm might be willing to provide testimony on Victor's violent temper. I wasn't sure though. I was afraid that instead of describing Victor as we knew him to be, Rita might choose to defend and praise her teacher. So I relied on Bernie to make that judgement call.

Rita was sworn in and Stephen Jackson began his questions.

"Tell us, Mrs. Robbins, you know the accused quite well, do you not?"

"I guess I do. We've been together in the quest for years, it seems. And we lived together, on the farm until Laura's tragedy."

"So you've observed her behavior over a period of years," Jackson said. "Could you say that there was anything violent in her nature."

"No. Never. Laura was fun loving and good natured, but never violent. Not when I knew her."

The cameras focused on Laura's face and I tried to guess what she was feeling, but I hadn't a clue. She sat unmoving and passive.

"And what was your relation to the deceased?"

"He was my teacher. He established a community called The Quest. That's where he taught us the esoteric meaning of life.

"And do you live in this community today?"

"Yes. I live in a Winnebago trailer, more or less permanently parked on the property. My two children attend the school there."

"And how long have you been involved with The Quest Mrs. Robbins?

"A little over four years."

"So you must have known LaMotta pretty well. What can you tell us about his character?"

"Well, first of all, he was a philanderer. Victor taught all of us in classes, but he also had private sessions with each of his students. Apparently, he tried to make love with many of the female students. We didn't used to talk about it. We each felt that we were the 'special' one. It came out gradually. I never knew that he had been sleeping with Laura Steiner."

"Tell us more about Victor Lamotta. Was he married?"

"Oh, yes. He was married, technically. I guess, he still is, or was. But when his wife found out that he was fooling around she kicked him out and ever since then he's been living with Gertrude Barry, she's the one his wife found out about. They have a baby together."

"What can you tell us about how he and Gertrude got along?"

"Oh, I can tell you all right. Victor was an abuser. No doubt about it, even if we didn't know it at first. Well, in class, sometimes he would belittle his students—make fun of their answers. But we thought that was just one of his teaching methods. Then, one day Gertrude came to lunch with ugly bruises all over her face. Did I tell you that we all used to eat together at the farm? So Gertrude is a mess and there was no way she could get out of telling us that Victor did it to her. It wasn't the first time either, but we didn't know it till then."

"Do you think Victor's history of abusive behavior is consistent with his attempting to rape Laura Steiner once she refused his advances?"

"Objection, your honor," Caleb Arnold called out. "This is leading the witness."

"Objection sustained. You will confine your questions to issues of fact, Mr. Jackson.

"Yes your honor. I have no further questions, Mrs. Robbins. Thank you."

Jackson sat down and Arnold rose to cross examine Rita.

"Mrs. Robbins, you said that you live in a Winnebago trailer and that your two children attend Victor Lamotta's school. With whom else do you live in that trailer, please?"

"With Al Kramer."

"Is he not your husband?"

"No."

"And are you divorced from your husband?

"No, but we are separated."

"I see," Arnold sneered, theatrically raising one eyebrow. "And were you, Mrs. Robbins, while living with this Kramer, were you ever intimate with Victor Lamotta?—Remember, you are under oath now."

Rita hesitated for a moment. Shifting her arms from the wooden arm rests of her chair, she clasped her two hands together, intertwining her fingers and rubbing her thumbs, one against the other. She looked over at Laura, holding her gaze for a moment. Rita was the first to look away. Then she turned towards the prosecutor and muttered "Yes."

"No further questions, your honor. You may step down, Mrs. Robbins."

The judge then announced, "As there are no further witnesses, we will take a break now and when we resume, in half an hour, if there are still no further witnesses we shall have summations from the two attorneys. I'm beginning to believe that this trial may be just as fast as the two attorneys told you it would be."

Louella got up from the couch and went to the bathroom. I went into the kitchen where I rummaged in the cabinets until I located a pack of potato chips. I tore it open and chomped a few and emptied the remainder into a plastic bowl.

Louella joined me in the kitchen saying, "Do you think it would be disrespectful to poor Laura if I were to pour us each a glass of wine and we should be comfortable while we watch the rest of the trial?"

"Who'll know?" I said.

We took our places back on the couch where we munched and sipped while a series of commercial messages filled the rest of the time until the trial resumed.

Caleb Arnold spoke first.

"All right, dear members of the jury, let me summarize, then, after you hear from the other side, you'll be able to bring this trial to a close whenever you're ready."

"You have a pretty clear picture, by now of what happened. What you need to keep in mind, as you deliberate is that these times we are living through aren't the most peaceful of times. America has enemies and they want to tear down our way of life. The woman whom you see here, on trial for murder, is one of those enemies. She is a professional trouble maker who opposes what America stands for."

"I don't want any of you good jurors to waste your tears over what happened to her that day in Cold Springs, Ohio when they were burning American flags. I can't imagine any one of you would thrust your own baby forward as a shield, defying your own government. Forget about that. We are not here to talk about what happened almost two years ago. We are here to convict this woman of murder."

Hearing this, and losing all restraint, I flung my potato chips at the television set. "You're a vicious, lying bastard!" I cried out.

"Calm yourself." Louella said, putting her arm across my body, holding me down in my seat.

The prosecutor strode over to the jury box, rested his hands on the railing, and continued.

"Now, there isn't any question that the accused, Laura Steiner, shot and killed Victor Lamotta. We know that. The question for you jurors to decide is why she did it. What was going on in her mind when she pulled the trigger, not once, but three times."

"It appears to me this is a very simple case, and I don't want to keep you good people here in this courthouse any longer than necessary."

"What I understand, and I'm confident you will see it the same way, is that this woman is consumed with hate. Whom does she hate? She hates everybody. She hates the country in which she was born. Probably she hates the father who gave her a child without ever giving it a name. There's a pretty good case to make for the idea that she even hated her very own child. Isn't there? Think about that for a moment.... "

The camera again focused on Laura. She was clearly angry. She made a motion to stand up and the policewoman at her side put an arm on her shoulder to restrain her.

The prosecutor went on:

"And when, on the night of March 15, she was confronted with the man who used to be her lover, she was so consumed with hate she shot him dead. She didn't shoot him once. She shot him three times."

"You've heard testimony they were lovers. No one is denying they were."

"So what happened on that night? The man, Victor Lamotta, now deceased, showed up, unexpectedly, at her door. She let him in."

"Who was this man? He had been her teacher once. It was way out mumbo jumbo, spiritual gobbldy-gook but apparently she believed whatever he was teaching her."

"Once inside her cabin, I suppose he tried to rekindle their old flame. We don't know for sure what happened next. What we do know is that after a while they were practically naked. We also know that later she took out her pistol and shot him, as I said, not once, but three times."

"The defense will take the stand, right after I finish and tell you that she shot in self defense, to prevent a rape. What you need to see clearly is that if she had time to go and get her gun, then she certainly wasn't being held down on the bed and having her clothes torn off of her. Was she?"

"Okay, visualize it. Somehow she has the pistol in her hand. A normal red blooded American woman, if she's trying to prevent a rape, might point it at the man, demand that he leave, and then lock the door behind him. Hell, excuse me, if she's really scared she might fire a warning shot. Or maybe shoot him in the leg. That'll cure his ardor."

"No. She didn't do any of those things. Laura Steiner shot him three times.—In anger. She knew exactly what she was doing. She made sure he was dead."

"And now, you, the jury will decide. Did Laura Steiner do what she did in order to preserve her already tarnished chastity? Or did she intentionally, snuff out the life of her teacher who had once been her lover?"

"I don't know, for sure, why she did it. Heck, nobody know for sure why anybody does anything. But I can make an educated guess and my best guess is that what motivated Laura Steiner was the same thing that seems to have been motivating most of her actions for years: hatred: deep, all consuming hatred: hatred for her country, hatred of men—all men, and, unfortunately, that means hatred for the man who had once been her teacher—and her lover."

"Do you follow me?"......."(long pause)

"Finally, I remind you, that if you find her guilty of murder, as charged, then it will be up to you jurors to decide on the penalty."

"Okay, that's it folks. I thank you for your attention and I thank you for doing your civic duty as good Americans."

As the prosecutor, Arnold, returned to his seat, the television camera focused on the jury box and I could see several of the jurors exchange nods and looks of approval.

Then we saw Stephen Jackson conversing with Bernie, who sat next to him. They shook hands and Jackson rose to speak for the defense.

He appeared to be confident as he smiled at the jury, examined them one by one before speaking, and then began.

"I too want to thank you all for serving on this jury. Yes, you have a momentous decision to make. But, unfortunately, the prosecution has sought to belittle your decision. He has suggested there isn't anything you need to think about. He asks for a quick verdict so you can hurry home to supper. So you can resume your lives as though the future of Laura Steiner's life is already pre-ordained. He suggests that the trauma Laura went through after leaving her home, here in Dallas and going off to college has nothing to do with this case. But you know very well, these are two events which cannot be separated."

"I am asking you to stop. Think. Put yourselves, even for a moment, into Laura's shoes. Who amongst you wouldn't be upset? Imagine, after the unspeakable horror of losing your child.... Suddenly, unexpectedly, a man who's presence is a reminder of the horrors which you are trying to escape from, he shows up at your door. You allow this old friend into your cabin and when you refuse his sexual advances he pounces on you, throws you to the bed and begins to tear off your clothing.—Not pleasant to imagine, is it?"

"Remember, it had been more than two years since Laura and her attacker had been intimate. Once upon a time, yes. But no longer. Lamotta was insistent. He was violent. You've heard, from Rita Robbins' testimony, he was a known abuser. Now he is upon her, crazed by his passion. Seeing that she was unable to defend herself in any other way Laura thought quickly. She told her attacker that she was willing to let him have his way with her, one more time. "Let me get up and put in my diaphragm," she said. He released her. She went to the bureau, rummaged in the drawer and took up her pistol. By the time she turned around Lamotta's pants and underpants were on the floor. Witnesses who came right after the shooting have attested, he had no pants on. She shot. Yes, three shots, to make sure that she was safe."

"That's how Lamotta was found. Lying on the floor, with no pants."

"It is important for you to know there is plenty of precedent here in the Dallas courts. I've been looking over the court records. You'd be surprised how many women have had occasion to shoot their lovers. I haven't found a single case but where the woman was judged to have done what was necessary and proper. So here we are.

All of us are Texans. We share a tradition of judging for ourselves what is right and what isn't. And none of us is afraid to assert that judgement, no matter how challenging the circumstances. I have full confidence you are going to find what Laura did in her moment of fear was what you might have done, and was certainly what you would have wished your daughters to have done."

"Thank you."

Steven Jackson returned to his seat, where Bernie Madison again shook his hand.

The judge then addressed the jury.

"You will now go into the jury room to deliberate. The state of Texas is charging Laura Steiner with willful murder. Laura Steiner is pleading "Not guilty of murder for reason of self defense."

"The court will await your verdict. And remember, if it is a verdict of 'guilty' then it is up to you, the jury, to assess the punishment."

Louella threw up her hands in astonishment.

"Is that it? Is it possible there isn't any more? Hasn't Bernie prepared anyone else? Only one witness? Why doesn't he let Laura speak for herself?"

"It's sort of a crapshoot." I answered.

I got onto my knees, began gathering up the potato chips strewn over the floor, and from my knees, I answered. "I knew she wasn't going to speak. Bernie told me last night. I'm sorry I didn't share it with you. That was dumb of me, but you were already asleep. What he said was that putting Laura on the stand could go either way. They both felt it would be dangerous. Maybe the jury would find her sympathetic, and maybe not. Maybe she could be made to appear as a bomb throwing anarchist. Nobody was sure."

"In fact, Bernie did have one more witness ready to go: a professor of psychology at SMU. The fellow was going to testify about the ways people respond to fear. He was going to make the case that Laura's behavior was neither unusual nor extreme."

"So why didn't he call the professor to the stand?"

"It turns out the man was a member of the American Civil Liberties Union. If the prosecution made him look like a radical he could have done our case more harm than good."

"Those people there are pre-historic!" Louella said.

"Don't you know it!"

"Get up from the floor, Mark. Come back to the couch and hold me. Hold me tight. Now I'm really scared."

I held her in my arms as we watched the jurors filing out of the courtroom. When the television screen switched from the courtroom to advertisements I suggested, "Let's drive out to the farm. I'm sure they're all watching too. You'll be of some comfort to Gertrude, Im sure. I'll hold Hannah's hand maybe."

We drove there and found the residents of the farm house in the big room, facing the television set, which was blaring out regional news. Gertrude was on the couch, nursing Victor Jr. Hannah sat in the overstuffed chair and was wrapped in an antique hand-stitched quilt. Patricia and Jeremy were at the table. Al wasn't there. He had accompanied Rita to Dallas for the trial.

As we entered Jeramy greeted us with a wave and a mock bow. "Welcome to our den of iniquities. We, the residents of Sodom and Gomorrah greet you."

"Shush. Don't make things even worse than they are," Patricia scolded her husband.

Louella and I each bent to kiss Hannah, then I joined Patricia and Jeremy at the table while my wife sat on the couch next to Gertrude and the baby. Louella put her arm around Gertrude and said, "I'm so sorry that you have to hear all this. You're living through something terrible, I know. But you'll come through it. I'm sure you will. We're all here to help you get through it."

"So?" I asked no one in particular. "Are they going to decide that she was just protecting herself—or will they throw the book at her?"

Most of us had no idea what the jury would decide. Only Hannah was convinced that things would be very bad for Laura.

In the midst of our conversation the program was interrupted.

"Here's breaking news." The screen switched back to the Dallas courtroom.

The jury had been conferring for only an hour. Now they filed in. When they were all seated the judge asked, "Have you reached a decision?"

"We have," said the foreman.

"And was it unanimous?" asked the judge.

"Yes, your honor. We find the defendant, Laura Steiner, guilty of willful murder as charged."

"Have you made a recommendation as to punishment?"

"We have. We recommend death by lethal injection."

"Is that it?" Louella asked.

Gertrude began to cry.

"Surely Bernie Madison will appeal," I suggested.

"Yeah," Jeremy said. "But who knows how that will turn out? When it comes to executions, the state of Texas is different from the rest of us...." His voice trailed off.

We all sat for a few moments, in silence. Then I got up and said, "Louella, let's go home." I turned to Hannah, "Do you want me to help you get upstairs before we go? Or are you comfortable down here?"

"No need for that, but thank you Mark. I can manage the stairs by myself, just fine now. Try to have a good evening. Or at least get yourselves some rest. This isn't the end. Things will sort themselves out in time. You'll see."

CHAPTER THIRTY-NINE

IN THE days that followed, organizations devoted to saving Laura's life sprang up everywhere and not just on campuses; student protest may have been the spark out of which the protests grew but now the religious communities were joining in. Her defenders became even more vociferous upon hearing that the higher courts had refused an appeal, declaring there was no legal basis for one.

Bernie remained in Dallas until he became convinced that all recourse had been exhausted. The verdict and the death sentence remained in place and Bernie returned to Cold Springs feeling defeated.

Now I heard from my old roommate, Jim Krikun. I was overjoyed when he telephoned, saying he would be in town on the weekend and hoped he could see us.

"What do you mean, 'See us'? You'll stay with us, won't you? Your old room is an office now but the couch opens up and you'll be comfortable on it. It'll be great to see you again!"

I'd carried a burden of guilt towards Jim ever since my wedding, when I let him drop out of my life and did nothing to stay in touch. Now his phone call eased some of that guilt. He was back, apparently with no ill feelings.

"No. But thanks for the invitation anyway," Jim said. "You won't have to put me up. I'm staying out at the farm. You know, The Quest. They have plenty of room for me. The main thing is, I want to thank the two of you for passing on my concerns to Gertrude. You guys made it happen. She invited me down. She hasn't changed all that much since she dumped me, took up with Victor, had a baby, and then had to face up to Victor's death. You know what? It's a terrible way to get out of a bad relationship, but I think Gertrude is feeling kind of relieved."

Student protest kept spreading.

Now that Bernie Madison was back from Dallas I arranged a meeting with President Hillestad.

Dean Lacy, Bernie and I filed in to the president's office on the ground floor of the administration building. I had been there only once before. The wooden paneling on the walls conveyed a feeling of seriousness. The overstuffed couches felt homey. President Hillestad had been in office for eight years already: longer than I had been on campus. He was considered to be a good administrator but the bulk of his work involved fund raising. He was the public face of the college and much of his time was spent traveling: visiting donors. This was the first time I met him since the day, seven years earlier, when my hiring became official as I was escorted into his office where he shook my hand and welcomed me to the faculty.

Dean Lacy opened the meeting.

"With your approval, Jim, we sent these two, our lawyer, Bernie Madison and Mark Green, out to Dallas for the explicit purpose of doing all they could to keep the name of Horace Mann College out of the news."

Bernie interrupted, "Fat chance of that happening!"

"Let me go on, Bernie. Your point is well taken though. Bernie and Mark did all that could be expected of them. But Horace Mann College is inextricably linked to these events and the whole country sees it that way. So now the time has come for us to do a turnabout. We have to do the right thing, not the safe thing. The country needs to see us taking a side, to speak out against the war—officially. Make it an institutional commitment. The massacre on our campus was horrible. Executing Laura Steiner would be one more horror. We've got to join in the movement to save her. It's the right thing to do. It may make it harder for you to go out and raise money for a while,

Jim, but our core supporters will applaud us for being true to our values and traditions. You'll see that I'm right."

"Whoa, slow down," said the president. "No need to lecture me. I understand your point. What are you suggesting we do?"

We strategized for a while. It was agreed that Bernie and Tom Lacy would prepare a statement setting forth the college's position opposing both Laura's death sentence and the war in Viet Nam. We all agreed that the two issues were linked: that in any other time or any other location, a death sentence would have been unthinkable.

I was given leave to travel for the next month: to address the same student rallies that Laura had been addressing. "Go there and speak as someone who knows her well. Louie can teach your classes. I've always wondered," President Hillestad said, "why our tiny lab school needs three teachers and a principal. Now he'll prove his worth. Right?"

The struggle was publicized worldwide. There were many more groups calling for me than I could possibly satisfy. The first time I faced a large audience it was an outdoor rally at Ohio State. I was terrified, but I recalled Victor's admonition to remain present and awake, to be conscious of myself and to let the words come in accord with the necessity of the moment. I took a deep breath, felt the weight of my body, and remembered who I was and why I was there. I looked around. In front of me were, I guessed, five or six hundred students, young men and women, some sprawled on the fresh May grass, many more standing, pressing up against the stage.

I mentally repeated Victor's teaching. *Be aware. Sense your presence. The words will come!* Then I began talking. It worked! The right words came of themselves and I thrilled at the enthusiastic applause following my speech. After that it became easier. For the next six weeks I spoke at so many rallies, on so many campuses that I could no longer keep track.

It was mid summer when, in response to the worldwide clamor, the Texas Governor, John Connolly, commuted Laura's death sentence to twenty-five years in prison.

Twenty-five years sounded harsh but all of us believed that once the war was ended Laura would no longer be demonized: she would be seen as the victim she was and be given a pardon.

I abandoned public speaking and returned to campus, preparing for the next term's teaching.

Hannah invited Louella and me to have dinner with her at the farm. We arrived, expecting to share the meal with all the farm's inhabitants but were surprised to see the table set for just three.

Responding to my look of puzzlement, Hannah explained:

"Gertrude," she said, "took the baby to Cleveland for the weekend. She's with Jim. If it works out as well as she is hoping she'll stay there. The last thing she told me is 'Be ready to pack up my things and send them on to me.' Patricia and Jeremy rented a house in town. They moved out yesterday. You know, they lost most of their enrollment at the time of the shooting. But Patricia told me that the school was really Victor's dream much more than her own. She'll find a job somewhere, I'd expect. I've asked Al and Rita to move the Winnebago someplace else. They didn't seem upset. They found another spot and plan to move there in the next week or so."

Louella embraced Hannah and said, "So it's happened! You've really got your farm back again. All to yourself. And by yourself. No courts. No jury trials. I'm so happy for you!"

"Congratulations!" I said beaming at Hannah and reaching out to shake her hand.

"No handshakes, you silly boy. Give me a kiss," she said.

I kissed Hannah on the cheek and then she hugged me, after which she said, "Come sit in the parlor. I'm going to fix us drinks before we eat and I have something to discuss."

We followed Hannah into the parlor where she poured a glass of white wine for Louella, and for the two of us, our accustomed martinis. As she handed each of us our drink I couldn't but notice the way she consciously made eye contact, as if to say, "I am happy to be serving you." This polite and pleasant behavior was one of the lessons that Victor had instilled in each of us and it had become automatic.

Still standing, Hannah said, "To health and happiness!" She clinked glasses with each of us. I reached across and clinked glasses with Louella.

"Now, here's what I have to say," Hannah continued. "I want the two of you to get out of that cramped prefabricated shack that you rent from the college... Right away! I want you to buy this farm from me. You'll come and live here. Don't tell me that you can't afford it. It will be cheap because part of the arrangement will include lifetime tenancy for me, whatever is left of my nearly used up life, that is."

Louella and I looked at each other and without exchanging a word it was clear that we each had the same thoughts. We stood up, simultaneously, Louella from the couch and I from an easy chair. We put down our glasses and hugged Hannah; we hugged each other, enjoying the warmth of a three way hug.

It happened astoundingly fast. We moved into the farm in mid-August, hardly able to believe our good fortune.

Our first morning on the farm I got up at dawn, without waking Louella, dressed, and went out to the barn to commune with my goat, Ruthie still in her summer quarters amongst the other goats, the sheep, and the chickens. This time Ruthie was in the company of her two kids, no longer young, but frisky and quite self sufficient.

"Ruthie," I said. "You're not just a boarder anymore. This is your home now."

I sniffed the barn scent, thinking that now I wasn't just a teacher. I was also a farmer. And then another thought came into my head. It came unbidden but caused me to quickly return home.

"Louella, wake up. Listen to me!"

"I'm already awake. I was just lying here."

"Louella, it's seven years already I've been teaching here. I'll bet they'll give me a sabbatical if I ask for it."

"Why would you want that?"

"Because I'm going to write, Louella. I'll write the book that Laura Steiner never finished. I'll write it for her."

Louella sat up in bed. Her look of concern gave way to a broad smile. "You know what? It's awfully late already to be applying for sabbaticals. But I'll bet you the college will love the idea!"

I went to see President Hillestad that morning and Louella was right.

I began by organizing the papers that Laura and I had accumulated in the past two years. *It won't be a senior thesis—That was then. But now I've got to tell her story for her.*

Louella was assigned three classes in the math department, but much of her time was spent developing the ideas she had brought back from Peekskill.

One afternoon, as I sat at my desk typing, Louella returned from town and came into the room. She stopped behind me, put her hands on my shoulders, kissed the back of my neck and asked, "I'm not interrupting your work am I?"

"Why?"

"Just wanted to tell you what the doctor confirmed. I'm pregnant."

Our daughter, Rachel, was born just a few months before my book was published. The timing of the book's release was excellent. Lyndon Johnson had escalated the war to the point where we had half a million troops fighting in Viet Nam. The bloody and increasingly unsuccessful war was being broadcast daily, in full color, steadily fueling the public's disillusion and disgust. My book was simply titled "Laura." It immediately became a best seller.

I arranged for the proceeds from the book to be divided equally: half for me and half for Laura.

When our daughter, Rachel, was three years old and off at day-care, Louella sat me down in the parlor with a request:

"Mark," she said. "You know how unhappy my poor father has been. Ever since he got out of prison and Mom wouldn't take him back into the house, it seems nothing has gone right for him. How would you feel if he came and stayed with us for a while?"

I looked around the room, across into the large dining room, out the window at the vegetable garden, and with very little hesitation said, "It's a good idea, Louella, this place is huge, you know, and it could use his green thumb."

It was a week after her father's arrival. Louella and I strolled out the lane, hand in hand, to meet the school van that brought our daughter home. Normally, the van would have deposited Rachel at our front door, but it was such a beautiful, Indian-summer's day that we savored the walk.

Arriving at the roadside mailbox, well ahead of the van, we had time to open and read the day's mail.

"Louella," I said, "It's here! Your letter from the software corporation. Here. Take it. You open it."

She grimaced, pulled her lower lip into her mouth, bit down on it, and delicately opened the envelope.

She read, and the concern gave way to joy.

"Yes!" she said. "They want to buy it! My computer language! Here. Read for yourself."

I took the letter from her and read. "My God! They're paying you so much more than my best seller ever earned!"

The van approached, stopped, and delivered our daughter. The three of us walked back down the lane,- Rachel in the middle, holding our hands and periodically we swung her in sweeping arcs. The sugar maple leaves were already turning. The warm sun pierced the already thinning canopy and the leaves sparkled. Behind the wooden slat fence we watched the grazing sheep, goats, and the two milk cows. We approached the vegetable garden. There were Hannah and Louella's father, on hands and knees, their heads practically touching. They were thinning the newest crop of radishes. "Lovely," I said.

Join us," said Hannah. "The garden needs cultivating."

www.ingramcontent.com/pod-product-compliance
Lightning Source LLC
Chambersburg PA
CBHW050356030726
47503CB00006B/1882